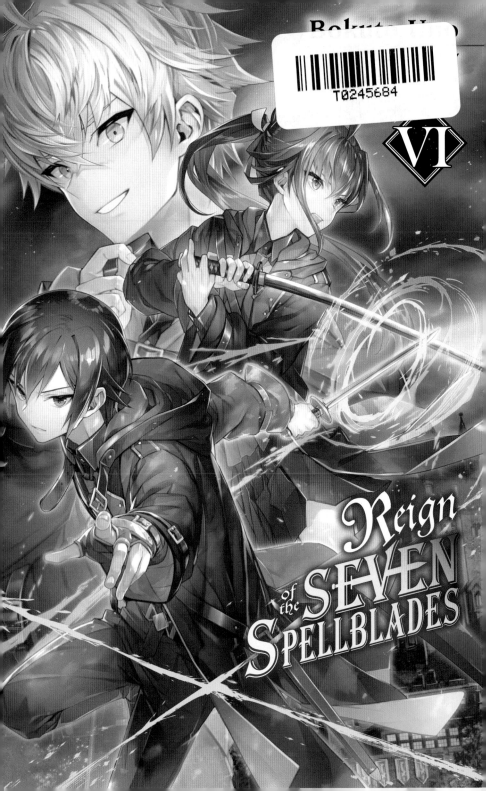

VI

Reign
of the SEVEN
SPELLBLADES

Oliver Horn

Michela McFarlane

Nanao Hibiya

This boy is super shady.

Yuri Leik

"I'm Yuri Leik, second-year. Just transferred to Kimberly from a nonmagical school."

"Let all voices cry out—we alone are fit to be the Kimberly Student Council!"

Leoncio Echevalria

Clifton Morgan

"Don't tell her I'm still alive."

"...I used to have a catcher of my own."

Diana Ashbury

CONTENTS

Reign of the Seven Spellblades
Bokuto Uno

Reign
of the SEVEN
SPELLBLADES

VI

Bokuto Uno

ILLUSTRATION BY
Ruria Miyuki

YEN ON
New York

Reign of the Seven Spellblades, Vol. 6
Bokuto Uno

Translation by Andrew Cunningham
Cover art by Ruria Miyuki

This book is a work of fiction. Names, characters, places, and incidents are the product of the author's imagination or are used fictitiously. Any resemblance to actual events, locales, or persons, living or dead, is coincidental.

NANATSU NO MAKEN GA SHIHAISURU Vol. 6
©Bokuto Uno 2020
Edited by Dengeki Bunko
First published in Japan in 2020 by KADOKAWA CORPORATION, Tokyo.
English translation rights arranged with KADOKAWA CORPORATION, Tokyo
through TUTTLE-MORI AGENCY, INC., Tokyo.

English translation © 2022 by Yen Press, LLC

Yen On
150 West 30th Street, 19th Floor
New York, NY 10001

Visit us at yenpress.com
facebook.com/yenpress
twitter.com/yenpress
yenpress.tumblr.com
instagram.com/yenpress

First Yen On Edition: August 2022
Edited by Yen On Editorial: Rachel Mimms
Designed by Yen Press Design: Andy Swist

Yen On is an imprint of Yen Press, LLC.
The Yen On name and logo are trademarks of Yen Press, LLC.

The publisher is not responsible for websites (or their content) that are not owned by the publisher.

Library of Congress Cataloging-in-Publication Data
Names: Uno, Bokuto, author. | Miyuki, Ruria, illustrator. | Keller-Nelson, Alexander, translator. | Cunningham, Andrew, translator.
Title: Reign of the seven spellblades / Bokuto Uno ; illustration by Ruria Miyuki ;
v. 1–3: translation by Alex Keller-Nelson ; v. 4–6: translation by Andrew Cunningham.
Other titles: Nanatsu no maken ga shihai suru. English
Description: First Yen On edition. | New York, NY : Yen On, 2020–
Identifiers: LCCN 2020041085 | ISBN 9781975317195 (v. 1 ; trade paperback) |
ISBN 9781975317201 (v. 2 ; trade paperback) | ISBN 9781975317225 (v. 3 ; trade
paperback) | ISBN 9781975317249 (v. 4 ; trade paperback) | ISBN 9781975339692
(v. 5 ; trade paperback) | ISBN 9781975339715 (v. 6 ; trade paperback)
Subjects: CYAC: Fantasy. | Magic—Fiction. | Schools—Fiction.
Classification: LCC PZ7.1.U56 Re 2020 | DDC [Fic]—dc23
LC record available at https://lccn.loc.gov/2020041085

ISBNs: 978-1-9753-3971-5 (paperback)
978-1-9753-3972-2 (ebook)

1 3 5 7 9 10 8 6 4 2

LSC-C

Printed in the United States of America

Characters

Second-Years

Oliver Horn

The story's protagonist. Jack-of-all-trades, master of none. Swore revenge on the seven instructors who killed his mother.

Nanao Hibiya

A samurai girl from Azia. Believes that Oliver is her destined sword partner.

Katie Aalto

A girl from Farnland, a nation belonging to the Union. Has a soft spot for the civil rights of demi-humans.

Guy Greenwood

A boy from a family of magical farmers. Honest and friendly. Has a knack for magical flora.

Pete Reston

A studious boy born to nonmagicals. Capable of switching between male and female bodies.

Michela McFarlane

Eldest daughter of the prolific McFarlane family. A master of the pen and sword, she looks out for her friends.

Tullio Rossi

A lone wolf who taught himself the sword by ignoring the fundamentals. Lost to Oliver in a duel.

Yuri Leik

A transfer student. What he lacks in sense, he makes up for in boundless curiosity. Chummy with everyone.

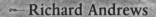

~ Richard Andrews   ~ Stacy Cornwallis

~ Fay Willock   ~ Joseph Albright

Fifth-Years

A witch who supports demi-human rights. Fought Oliver and his friends over Katie but has since taken an interest in the group.

Vera Miligan

Kimberly's top broomsport athlete. Nanao's broomriding skills catch her attention.

Diana Ashbury

Sixth-Years

Student council president. Nicknamed Purgatory by his peers. Boasts incredible firepower.

Alvin Godfrey

A gentle girl and Oliver's cousin. Supports Oliver's secret activities as his vassal.

Shannon Sherwood

Ashbury's former catcher. Easygoing and intrepid. His research has left him consumed by tír fire.

Clifton Morgan

A quiet young man and Oliver's cousin. Supports Oliver's secret activities as his vassal.

Gwyn Sherwood

Leader of the previous student council's faction. Once battled Godfrey for the presidency and received burns to the right side of his face, which he refuses to heal.

Leoncio Echevalria

First-Years

Oliver's closest vassal, aiding his revenge as a covert operative. Moves on her own terms and shows few emotions.

Teresa Carste

Instructors

Kimberly's headmistress. Proudly stands at the apex of magical society.

Esmeralda

Magical engineering instructor. Prone to outrageous lessons designed to maim students.

DECEASED

Enrico Forghieri

Chela's father and the man who sent Nanao to Kimberly.

Theodore McFarlane

Magical biology instructor. Feared by her students for her wild personality.

Vanessa Aldiss

- Demitrio Aristides
- Frances Gilchrist
- Luther Garland
- Dustin Hedges
- Darius Grenville DECEASED

CHAPTER 1

§

The Stranger

The faces of students entering a classroom provide a valuable clue as to the subject of the class ahead. If the stressed-to-excited ratio was one to one, it was sword arts. Two to one, spellology.

But for *this* class, the ratio was between fear and grim determination, at a mere one to four.

"Is everybody ready?" Chela said, glancing at each of her friends in turn. All five nodded wordlessly. They had long since adapted to this tension. It was part and parcel with Enrico Forghieri's magical engineering class.

"...Let's hope everyone keeps their limbs today," Guy replied.

"That depends on the assignment," Pete said, not looking up from his book.

Surprised by the lack of emotion, Katie leaned in. "...You're awfully calm, Pete. These classes used to leave you shaking."

"Whatever he throws at us, our approach is the same. Observe, analyze, and handle it as best we can. Nothing else to it."

Pete snapped his book shut. A grating laugh echoed through the door, and every student braced themselves. A moment later, the door burst open, and a little old man sailed in.

"Kya-ha-ha-ha-ha-ha! Good morning, children! Today's assignment...will have to wait, I'm afraid."

Enrico stopped at the podium, pausing dramatically. The students had been ready to put their lives on the line and did not know what to make of *this*.

"First, a very important announcement: ...I'm dead! Actually, legitimately deceased!"

There was a *clank*, and Enrico's jaw slid downward, flipping like a ventriloquist's dummy. A terrifying sight that stunned every student present.

"...Um?" Pete said, his voice shaking.

But this thing *shaped* like Enrico continued prattling away. "What you see before you is merely a dummy golem. Designed to activate automatically if I fall out of contact for a set period of time. No one has verified my body, but circumstantial evidence suggests a high likelihood I have met with an untimely demise! Proceed accordingly. Kya-ha-ha-ha-ha!"

As he explained further, his eyeballs popped out, bouncing on the ends of springs. The goofball visuals were so removed from the grim nature of the facts at hand that no one present could process the news. And yet—it made *sense*. The mad old man would hardly shed a tear over his own expiration.

"But still your beating hearts! This golem is fully equipped to conduct class. It may lack my creative panache, but I have filled it to the brim with my vast reserves of knowledge. Rest assured, this class is in capable hands. You will hardly notice the difference!"

"Er, um..." Pete shot to his feet.

Dummy Enrico pushed his eyes back into his face and beamed at him.

"You have a question, Mr. Reston?"

"Y-you died, but...how?"

Pete was definitely speaking for everyone.

"That's under investigation," the golem said, hands out wide. "But indeed, *who killed me*? That is the question on all our minds."

The mechanical old man cackled with delight, and Pete just stared, aghast. Behind him, Chela turned to the boy beside her.

"...Oliver, what do you make of it?"

The boy folded his arms and grimly shook his head. They knew too little, and careless speculation would do no one any good. His expression spoke for him.

The crease on his brow, the slight incline of his head—every gesture the spitting image of Oliver Horn, deep in thought.

Meanwhile, on the labyrinth's first layer—the quiet, wandering path— in the Sherwoods' secret atelier.

"——AaaaaAAAAAAAAAAAAAAAAAAAAAAA!"

A boy's screams echoed ceaselessly through a soundproof room.

His future hung in the balance. Oliver was strapped to an operating table, struggling with all his might, entirely out of his mind. Left to his own devices, he would destroy his own body. To prevent that, every comrade with healing skills was here, and his cousins were on a sleepless vigil.

"Inject a triple dose of red spotweed anesthetic! Apply a seventy-percent paralysis spell on the tendons of every limb! Hurry! He's about to blow!"

"……!"

It would be so much easier if they could just put him to sleep. But the rejection from a soul merge was nothing so mild that sleep would help—quite the opposite. He *had* to fight off the haphazard spasms with his mind alert and conscious. Oliver was in the throes of a battle for his life.

Those who wished to aid him had only two options available: protect his body, ensuring this struggle did not damage it permanently, and use spells and magic herbs to ease the pain wherever possible. With those tasks handled flawlessly, there was little left to do but have faith in Oliver himself. His battle had raged for three days and nights, and all they could do was watch.

"Take a rest, Gwyn," a comrade said.

Gwyn's fatigue was more than evident. He was running on zero sleep, and it had been a good twelve hours since he'd last eaten anything, much less had a sip of water. Aware that this path led only to his own collapse, Gwyn stepped away from the table.

"...I'm gonna go splash some water on my face. Shannon, let someone else take over. You need rest."

She was on the other side of the table from him, but her only response was a vehement shake of her head. Gwyn knew full well nothing he could say would change her mind, so he let her be and left the operating room, headed for the sinks next door. He had the attending elemental generate water so cold, it was almost ice and splashed it on his face to wake himself.

"...This is rough."

He looked up from the sink to find a girl standing next to him. One of their number. Like him, a sixth-year student—Janet Dowling.

Listening to the screams from the next room, she spoke again.

"Three days since the fight, and he's still not stabilizing. This soul merge thing is gnarly."

"........."

"Not that you're faring much better, though. You look about ready to hang yourself."

She reached out and pulled his chin to face her. There was a moment of silence, and then she smirked.

"Take a load off," she said, her tone suddenly far softer. "I know you don't want to hear it, but torturing yourself isn't gonna ease your cousin's pain."

Gwyn silently pushed her hand away and got back to washing his face.

Janet changed the subject. "How's the cover-up going? Not just the battle site but our lord himself. He's been absent from class for three days, right?"

"We've got a double in his place. Should work for the time being. The longer this drags on, the more we'll have to consider alternatives..."

When the cold had turned his lips blue, Gwyn finally stopped. He grabbed a towel and dried his face.

"As for the site of the battle, that's at a critical juncture. We've eliminated all evidence that'll directly tie it to any of us, but there's no hiding Enrico's disappearance. We'll need to concoct a cover story."

"Like that he was consumed by the spell?"

"That would be the obvious choice. A Deus Ex Machina is absolutely the sort of project that harbors that threat. But that won't be enough to fool Kimberly's staff."

Gwyn scowled at his reflection in the mirror. His exhaustion was plain as day, yet his eyes had already turned toward the battle ahead.

"Like with Darius, when a teacher here dies, the first suspects are always other instructors. For the simple reasons that they are the most likely to be capable of it. And that works to our advantage—we'll sow the seeds of doubt."

"And potentially turn them against one another," Janet said, jumping ahead of him.

Gwyn nodded. "We need them taking each other out. Noll can't handle more fights like this one."

His fist was clamped so tight, the bones in his hand creaked. Janet's eyes narrowed. Perhaps this man's heart would give out before his cousin's body.

"Subterfuge, huh?" She grinned. "Sounds fun."

Gwyn made to answer but felt a presence behind him. He turned and found a covert operative standing uneasily, seemingly unsure of what to do with herself.

"Why are you here, Teresa? I told you not to come."

He shot her a stern look, and she mouthed a few words before managing to vocalize anything.

"…Just…one look…"

"You want to see Noll spitting blood, writhing in agony?"

The girl flinched. He showed no mercy.

"There is nothing you can do here. Return to campus and remain in class until you receive other orders. That is your mission."

"………"

"Answer."

"......Mission received."

Teresa was frowning, not even trying to hide her frustration. She turned and left the room.

"...I really *felt* that frustration," Janet said, fascinated. "Since when has she been all emotional like that?"

"She's changed a lot since she first met Noll. I suppose that means she cares about him...as best she can."

His voice had softened a tad.

Janet groaned lightly, rolling her neck. "That's adorable, but not ideal. Is our lord feeling anything back? Will he be able to sacrifice her if the need arises?"

"I have no intention of putting that choice before him."

There was such steel in his voice that she flinched, then threw up her hands.

"Doing his dirty work for him. Like brothers everywhere. How noble."

She gave him a slap on the back, then headed for the door. He watched her go.

Janet's smile was indomitable—almost diabolically so.

"Good, good. You won't be the only ones with dirt on your hands. This next stage is *our* job as Kimberly's third-rate rag!"

Well-fed citizens crave *information*. Mage or not, this is a fundamental human instinct.

"Hokay, how do we frame it, Chief?" a reporter said, licking the end of their pen.

A tiny space packed with desks. The desks and floor were covered in notes, documents, and photos.

Kimberly students ran multiple papers, and thus there were several press clubs. This one was headquartered inside the labyrinth.

"Hmm, how's this?" they said, showing off a headline. "Pretty dang inflammatory, but that's kind of our thing."

"Oh-ho-ho-ho! That ought to piss *everyone* off," another reporter said, rubbing their hands together.

The mock-up had, in huge letters, ENRICO MISSING! INFIGHTING AT KIMBERLY?! scrawled across the top. Like any good tabloid, this one stirred the pot with no regard for ethics. Treating the incident as a murder before any facts were out and pinning the blame on faculty conflicts—transparently biased reporting.

"...Psh. Weak," Janet snapped. She waved her white wand, erasing those letters, and filled the blanks with words of her own. The reporters looked aghast.

"...Uh..."

"Whoa..."

"I'd go with this," Janet said, turning around. All eyes were on the board behind her.

WHO IS THE COLLEAGUE KILLER?! SECRET STRIFE AMONG THE KIMBERLY FACULTY!

Everyone gulped.

"The chief's lost it..."

"Oh-ho-ho! Coming on *strong*!"

This would be published. The faculty would see it. That idea alone sent a chill down their spines. But none of them tried to stop her. The article's accuracy was irrelevant—Kimberly's third-largest paper existed for one thing and one thing only: sticking it to the man.

"You guys need me to remind you what we're all about? One hundred and twenty years of being the trashiest rabble-rousing rag around. We can't let *this* shit go unstirred!"

Their article was in ink that very day, spread to every corner of the campus right as crowds began to form.

"Extra, extra! Latest news on Enrico's disappearance!"

Desperate for information, students snatched up copies for themselves. Eighty percent of the article was entirely baseless speculation, but that fueled vehement arguments. This was no longer "Enrico's disappearance." The whole discussion had been shifted, and everyone was talking about who the Colleague Killer could be.

Two AM. After a long struggle and an ensuing coma, Oliver's eyes slowly opened.

"............————"

For several seconds, he was at a loss. His body *wasn't* racked with pain. At this point, that felt far stranger. He looked around and found himself no longer on the operating table but on a proper bed with clean sheets. His sister was on a chair next to the bed, clutching his hand, nodding off.

"...Shannon," he said, sitting up.

Her eyes snapped open, focusing on him. "...Noll...you're awake...!"

She'd clearly been crying a lot, and now fresh tears welled up. She threw herself onto him, wrapping her arms around him tightly and sobbing in his ear. That alone proved just how bad things had been, and it left him at a loss for words.

Eventually, he managed to ask, "...How many days has it been?"

"Four days and twelve hours," Gwyn answered as he entered the room. "Acceptable range. Go back to sleep."

He came over to the bed. His fatigue was undisguisable, but relief was winning out. Relief that Oliver had woken up intact.

"Anything feel strange or out of place?"

Making no attempt to pry Shannon loose, Oliver turned inward, feeling himself out. His limbs were limp—lingering anesthetic. Otherwise, nothing noticeably amiss. But *"strange"*—well, that described every part of him, down to the tips of his fingers.

"No...pain. Just... It all feels wrong. Like every part of me's been replaced," he said, picking his words.

Gwyn nodded. "It has. This soul merge induced a clear physical change. You're nearly an inch taller. Muscles, bones, organs, and mana flow—there's gonna be countless little changes all over."

"........."

"We'll monitor your progress with it. There's a lot we don't know about the physical side effects of a lengthy merge. But there's one thing I can say for sure—"

"—I carved a huge chunk off my life?"

These words made Shannon tighten her embrace. Oliver winced. He knew only too well how she felt, but at this rate, he'd never get moving.

"Let me try it out. Shannon, if you could—"

"No."

"Please...?"

"No!"

Each time she refused, her embrace grew tighter. With the anesthetic lingering, he wasn't capable of pushing her off, and he would never have done that to his sister in the first place.

Seeing his little brother helpless, Gwyn shot him a grin.

"All right, you two just sleep together here. She hasn't slept a wink since."

"S-sleep...in the same bed?"

"Not necessarily, but good luck peeling her off you."

Clearly, Gwyn knew better. Oliver put an arm around his sister and lay back down. Gwyn put a blanket over them both and turned to go.

"Let us love you. It's how we get through this."

And with that, he was gone, leaving Oliver and Shannon pressed tight against each other. Shannon adjusted their positions under the covers, pulling his head against her chest. His nostrils caught a sweet scent, and his heart almost leaped out of his chest.

"Hee-hee. It's been so long…since we slept together."

"………"

"And you're still…very red."

He couldn't really move, but he did his best to turn his face away. Shannon just smiled at him…and then felt something by her hips and peeked inside the blankets.

"That…hasn't changed, either."

"……!"

All too aware of his shame, Oliver looked ready to cry. He normally had these involuntary responses under complete control, but since he'd just been through the fight of his life, the drugs in his system weren't allowing that. He tried to pull his hips away, but Shannon was holding on tight, not letting him flee. Heedless of the stiffness pressed against her.

"No you don't. Sleep. Sleep right here…with me."

The inappropriate urge soon faded in the warmth of his sister's embrace and the relief it brought. She gave him no choice, so he surrendered to her love…and before he knew it, Oliver was asleep again.

It was a full five hours before he woke once more. He left Shannon sleeping like the dead and found a sink, washing his face and making himself presentable. By way of self-evaluation, he ran through a few movements and spells. The precision left much to be desired; it felt like he was controlling someone else's body entirely. But he'd trained through these sensations at a much younger age, and it likely wouldn't take too long to adjust.

Nothing to worry about. Just as he was wondering when to return to school, someone spoke the password, and the atelier door opened. In came…Oliver himself, a flawless match, from the clothes to the face. The double who'd filled in for him during his absence. A fourth-year named Theo Jeschke. Their true age and gender were unclear—in fact, almost everything about them was shrouded in mystery.

"Welcome back. No trouble filling in for you on my end."

"...Good. That's a huge help."

Theo spoke a spell and shifted into a new form before his very eyes. Oliver's gratitude was genuine. Post-transformation, Theo appeared to be a rough-and-tumble gal, but that was likely not their true face. Even Oliver had no clue what they'd originally looked like.

"Well, while we celebrate, let me run you through impressions and updates. Everything you need to know about my time doubling for you."

Theo took charge without even bothering to ask Gwyn for permission, sitting cross-legged on a table and waving Oliver to the seat opposite. He obliged.

"Gut reaction: Being you is damn hard. You're close with a bunch of your peers, which makes it extra tricky to avoid giving myself away. That's not a criticism! I'm actually impressed. Not everyone can build bonds that meaningful."

They let out a long sigh, then continued.

"All your friends are forces to be reckoned with. Especially the samurai girl. Every time she fixed her eyes on me, I felt a chill run down my spine. Granted, as long as I'm transformed, nobody can tell."

This, Oliver agreed with. Nanao's gaze was a force to be reckoned with.

"But remember this—the ironclad law of transformation. No matter how good you are, you can't ever *become* someone else. Not even a dazzling talent like myself. There's always something you can't quite hide and gotta talk your way out of or cover up the best you can. And the longer I'm standing in, the greater the risk of discovery. Situationally dependent, of course."

Oliver nodded, accepting all these warnings.

Theo grinned, folding their arms. "That said, a few days ain't gonna pose a real threat. Call me when you need it. As for what you're supposed to know…"

Before Oliver headed back up, he needed a full briefing on every conversation Theo had had while covering for him. This took a good fifteen minutes. Once fully prepped, he thanked them again and turned to go.

"Oh, wait. One more thing," Theo called. "No swapping during exam periods without a *really* good reason. You've gotta pass those yourself, kiddo."

"I plan to," Oliver said, grinning.

Then he left his cousins' atelier and headed out into the labyrinth beyond. With memories of his brutal fight still raw, banter like that really helped take his mind off things. His double knew how to manage people's emotions, too. And that made Oliver's steps all the more assured.

"Oh, there you are, Oliver."

"The mutton ribs are truly magnificent this morning!"

He met up with his friends for supper. Business as usual for them, but for Oliver, it had been several days, and he'd spent those staring death in the face. He sat down, keeping those emotions at bay. Then he took a sip of the tea Chela handed him and looked around.

"…Feels tense in here," he said.

"All because Instructor Enrico disappeared. The paper's extra edition spread like wildfire, and now few people are talking about anything else."

Chela had a copy of it on the table even as she spoke. Oliver glanced down at it and frowned. WHO IS THE COLLEAGUE KILLER?! was certainly a provocative headline. He immediately knew which paper was responsible. The editor in chief was a comrade, and this must have been part of their disinformation campaign: baiting the student body into believing the faculty had turned against one another.

Glancing around at the gossiping students, Chela sighed. "Last year, there was Darius, so this makes it two years straight. It's no wonder speculation is so rampant."

"Shit's not funny," Guy said. "Student scuffles make this place dangerous enough, and now we've got teachers killing each other?"

"...But *are* they?" Katie asked.

"Opposing viewpoints, the urge to pursue your own sorcery—it's hardly unusual for mages to find themselves fighting to the death. But Kimberly faculty are a different story," Chela explained. "If the students here are fish, then the instructors are the tank that holds us. They are what allows us to swim freely through the campus, and should that break down, there would be nothing left but chaos. I certainly hope this article is entirely meritless...not least because my father would be right at the center of it."

She concluded on a grim note.

Pete had been thinking hard this whole time, and he finally spoke. "...If the culprit *isn't* a teacher, what then?"

"An accident in the labyrinth's depths or consumed by the spell doing one experiment too many. Those are the most likely explanations, but for that to happen two years in a row strains credulity."

"No way a student did it." Guy scowled. "The teachers here are all *beasts*."

Chela's frown deepened. She locked her fingers together.

"And both missing teachers served on the front lines of the Gnostic hunts. Even a team of the best upperclassmen likely wouldn't fare well. Hypothetically speaking, at my current abilities, a hundred of me wouldn't stand a chance against my father. That's a simple fact."

Oliver nodded quietly. He knew full well that was no exaggeration.

A silence settled over the table, so Chela brought the discussion to a close.

"Either way, this is no ordinary situation. The headmistress will be forced to take action. And once the witch of Kimberly is motivated, no crisis will last for long."

Meanwhile, in a third-floor meeting room, the Kimberly faculty were in session.

"State your views."

The silver-haired witch sat at the narrow end of an elliptical table— the closest thing to a throne this school had.

The tyrant to her right was the first to respond.

"Views, my ass," she snarled. "Someone here did it."

This was the magical biology instructor, Vanessa Aldiss. She'd been dead sure another teacher had killed Darius, and that opinion hadn't wavered in the meantime.

"Don't be absurd, Ms. Aldiss," scoffed the man across the table from her. "What would be the point of that?"

This was the broomriding instructor, Dustin Hedges. Vanessa shot him her fiercest glare, but before she could respond, the teacher to Esmeralda's left chimed in.

"I agree with Dustin. Kimberly is an ideal home for any mage. I find it hard to believe any of us would choose to wreck that."

The speaker wore a dapper brown suit—Theodore McFarlane, part-time lecturer. Like Dustin, he clearly thought the colleague-killer theory was entirely without merit.

"One fact is clear. Darius and Enrico have both vanished," said a man in old-fashioned robes. "And I think it highly unlikely that instructors just happened to be consumed by the spell two years running. On that, I am sure we all agree."

Demitrio Aristides, astronomy instructor.

"There is a threat somewhere on campus," an elderly witch added, nodding. "Foe or foes, this enemy has the strength to take on those two warlocks. Our discussion should proceed with that assumption in mind."

Frances Gilchrist taught spellology and had lived for more than a thousand years. Her words had weight, and a long silence followed them.

A timid voice broke it. "W-we might be worried about nothing. Perhaps both Darius and Enrico could come strolling back in tomorrow..."

This strained croak came from the plump woman at the far end of the table, the school librarian, Isko Liikanen. Since she was not a teacher, few took what she said to heart. Several present were openly smirking.

"Fair enough, Isko," the teacher next to her said. "Part of me feels the same way. If only they were both safe and sound! But right now, we need to make plans on the assumption that they aren't."

Darius had been the alchemy instructor, and this was his replacement—Ted Williams. Even this soft response was enough to make the librarian lower her head.

A deep voice cut in. "Don't care who did it. Only care if my flower beds get messed up."

The man's gloomy scowl scanned the faces present. He taught a magical biology specialty course dealing only with magiflora. His bangs hung low like so much shrubbery, and he looked less like a teacher than an ornery gardener fending off interlopers.

"Bring me a body, and I can do summat wit' it," snapped a woman with blunt-cut blond hair. Kimberly's school physician, Gisela Zonneveld. Lord of the campus infirmary, she'd reattached countless student limbs and stuffed their guts back inside their bodies. It took a lot to make her leave that post—according to the woman herself, *"If they can't get ta the infirmary, they're dead anyway."*

The more faculty members spoke, the tenser the room got. A teacher near the center rose to his feet, his voice ringing out above the grumbling.

"No need to get ahead of ourselves. Unlike with Darius, this time, we have evidence. Let's begin by reviewing it."

Luther Garland. Clad in white robes, he was the sword arts

instructor. His gaze fell to the table where Enrico Forghieri had once sat—and where a golem made in his image now resided.

"Dummy Enrico, will you elaborate?"

"Kya-ha-ha-ha-ha! With pleasure."

The cheery golem bent over backward, and his chest split open vertically. A quadruped golem clambered out, scuttling across the table and stopping at the center. There was a pyramid-shaped crystal on top of the golem; it lit up, projecting a 3D image of elsewhere.

The faculty were now looking at a rocky landscape on which lay the body of an immense golem.

"...Fifth layer," Demitrio said. "Just outside Hall Eleven?"

"Talk about getting your ass beat!" Vanessa cackled. "That's the old man's precious Deus Ex Machina, right? Or what's left of it!"

Ted leaned in, inspecting it closely. "Only major damage is to the head. Melted via extreme heat, I suppose?"

"Melt marks on the right palm, too!" the dummy said. "High odds it was downed by the power of its own spirit light."

Dummy Enrico zoomed in to show the palm and head in close-up.

Examining these thoroughly, Dustin said, "Honestly, at a glance, it looks like he lost control of the golem during activation."

"Poppycock," Gilchrist snapped. "The boy would never make such a silly mistake."

Everyone scowled at the projection. "...Zoom in on the torso," Garland said.

The dummy did as requested, giving them a better view of the countless scratches on the adamant armor.

"Claw marks," Theodore muttered. "Given the location: wyverns? The lindwurm?"

"Something about that bugging you, Garland?" Vanessa asked.

Dragon claws were among the hardest things around; they could easily scratch adamant like this. Garland was well aware of that, but he still stared for a long moment before answering.

"…No, I can't see anything out of place."

He broke off his search, falling silent.

"Ms. Muwezicamili is securing the scene," the dummy added. "Given the size and the location, recovering the construct will take a while. If we find any further clues, I'll make sure everyone hears."

"Please do," Theodore said. "It is our one tangible lead."

The smaller golem ended the projection and moved toward Esmeralda, offering itself up as evidence.

One eye on the witch of Kimberly's steely profile, Theodore changed tactics.

"However, it seems we are without actionable clues. Which means we have our work cut out for us, Headmistress."

At this prompt, Esmeralda intoned, "Conduct a school-wide investigation."

Everyone looked tense. Demitrio voiced the obvious question. "To what degree?"

"Primary and secondary would be tricky," Theodore said. "At this stage, the best we can manage is tertiary."

Esmeralda's silence on the subject signaled agreement.

The Kimberly witch added, "Use the estimated time of the incident to formulate a list of potential suspects. Teachers, students, and all other staff included. I will personally speak to anyone on that list deemed noteworthy."

Clearly, she meant business. And every instructor here was acutely aware that any actions they took during this investigation would be under the utmost scrutiny. With a faculty member as the most likely suspect, flushing them out was the goal.

"Good plan," Theodore said, ignoring the rising tensions. "But given the size of the school, we can hardly handle everything ourselves. There are any number of ways to skirt our attentions. As I'm sure you're all aware."

"State your point," Esmeralda growled.

The ringlet instructor winked at her. "I've already planted someone. Inside the student body."

"So good! Gosh, what a feast!"

A loud voice rang out above the dinnertime hubbub in the Fellowship.

"This is so not fair! You've all been dining like this the whole time?! No wonder everyone from Kimberly grows up so strong! Food is life! Life is power! That's just fundamental! Other schools could learn a thing or two."

Oliver's group looked up from their meals. Chattering away to no one in particular, a male student was drifting between tables, a plate in each hand. Anytime he found a new dish, he piled more on, and each plate already had quite a mountain.

His uniform indicated he was a second-year, but no one present had seen him before. Anyone who stood out like this would be hard to forget.

"Anybody got an empty seat? I seem to have arrived at peak dining rush! Oh dear. Oh dear! I can't just come back later; I've already got too much food! And I'm *starving*."

He made a huge show of looking around, and several students hastily averted their gazes before they made eye contact. The boy was left table-less. Oliver's group glanced at one another, collecting opinions from looks alone. These ranged from *Weirdo. Don't bother* to *Poor kid. Let him sit.*

Chela tabulated these silent votes and turned to the boy.

"...Excuse me—you there. We've got a spare seat."

"What, really?! Ha-ha-ha! I was just talking to myself, but it looks like you happened to hear!"

The boy dashed over to them, plopping his two heaping plates down on the table.

He pressed a hand to his chest theatrically.

"I'm Yuri Leik, second-year. Just transferred to Kimberly from a nonmagical school," he said. "Kind strangers, I'm sure we're going to be friends! Please, may I have your names?"

This introduction made their opinion unanimous: *This boy is super shady.*

CHAPTER 2

Hidden Struggles

A top broomsports player once said: *"The faster you fly, the fewer people you have around you."* That isolation is more frightening than anything—worse than the pressure to set a new record, worse than the risk of any fall.

"...*Hahhh...!*"

Words every broomrider knew but few experienced for themselves. The witch rocketing across the practice field was one of those few. The howl of the wind snatched away all other sounds, the view streaming past her blinkered vision too fast to see. She was in a world of her own—not even metaphorically.

"...Yo, Ashbury! Break—!"

A teammate yelled up at her, but the wall between their worlds batted his words aside. Her back was to him before he could even finish. The Blue Swallows shook their heads.

"...See? She ain't listening. Can't even hear us."

"I dunno how she stays that focused. She's been at it for five hours! The catchers are dead tired. We've gotta make her stop or..."

They turned around, looking at the girl behind them: a second-year student in a Wild Geese uniform.

"Welp, there you have it. I reeeally hate to ask, but can you step in, Ms. Hibiya?"

The Azian girl nodded with quiet authority and mounted her broom. "I give my word—assuming I can even catch the lady."

She looked up at Ashbury again and took several deep breaths, heightening her focus. Then Nanao kicked the ground, and she was in the air. Her launch alone was at top speed, and she was only getting faster. Far more technically proficient than she'd been a year before, she had the crowd of players below crossing their arms and groaning.

"Hrm...!"

But even at her speed, catching the Blue Swallows' ace would be a tall order. Two or three laps of the field would not be enough to get anywhere close to her velocity. There was a grin on Nanao's face. She couldn't even catch Ashbury's shadow. The technical gap was a *gulf*.

"*Hahhh......!*"

And that was *why* this chase was so much fun. Her mana running high, turning her black hair white, she poured everything she had into her beloved broom, Amatsukaze, flying faster still. Five laps, six, seven, eight, each lap's time shrinking. The players below gulped, and the catchers on standby grew tense. She was far beyond speeds any underclassman should be capable of.

However—that also meant Nanao had one foot inside the world of the witch ahead. Ashbury registered her presence and slowed her broom, adjusting her trajectory so that she and the Azian girl were flying side by side. The ground crew cheered. It had taken Nanao twelve laps to make contact.

"What do you want, Ms. Hibiya?" Ashbury asked from right beside her.

Barely maintaining this speed, Nanao responded, "I would have words with you. What say you to a landing, Ms. Ashbury?"

"Some other time. I'm too busy to play with you."

And with that, Ashbury sped up, easily leaving Nanao behind. The crowd let out a moan, but Nanao did not give up. She aimed to fly as long as she had the strength within her—and a lap later, as they lined up once more, she slid alongside Ashbury.

"Yet, you know full well play is a necessity."

"...Give it up."

Paying her no attention, Ashbury sped straight on by. She likely intended that as outright rejection, but Nanao saw it in a very different light—to her, this simply meant she could get a word in each time Ashbury passed her. She need only pile those on until her rival's mind changed, even if it took a thousand tries.

And she stuck to that plan. Lap after lap, speed never wavering, calling out each time Ashbury drew near. Bones creaking from combatting the inertia and g-forces at each turn, biting the flesh of her cheeks when her consciousness threatened to slip away, flying on and on all for the sake of a second's repartee.

"In my land...we say: *'In a hurry? Look around!'*"

"......"

Ashbury ignored her, flying on—but then she bit her lip. The Azian girl's steadfast determination spoke more than any words. How much strength was this girl using for this fragmented back-and-forth? What kept her going?

And she was still thinking on it when Nanao caught up once more, clearly well past her limits and barely clinging on to her broom.

"...Perchance...a moment of respite...?"

"......Argh, fine!"

Ashbury threw in the towel. She turned off her course, and Nanao followed. Their two brooms traced an arc toward the ground below.

"Have it your way! But ten minutes! No more."

"...The honor is mine," Nanao managed.

A few seconds later, the players on the ground cheered their arrival—and Nanao collapsed in a heap.

In short, a lack of blood flow to the brain. High-speed maneuvers took their toll on the circulation, and incidents like this were all too common among broomriders. The players knew what to do, and she was soon resting in the breeze beneath a tree.

"Here. Drink this."

"Much appreciated..."

Nanao was flat out on her back, so Ashbury gently poured the contents of the vial down her throat. She gulped away and finally managed to catch her breath.

"Hmph," the older girl said. "You're a decade away from matching me in a time attack."

"Indeed, I am not yet capable of keeping up... Truly prodigious speed."

Nanao meant every word. The back she'd pursued had been a distant target.

Ashbury planted herself next to her. "Naturally. Broom wars and broom races just demand far greater speed than anything else. Brooms are capable of speeds the human body cannot withstand— even a mage. You need a body *built* for that purpose from the moment of your birth."

"From birth, you say?"

Nanao turned her gaze, inspecting the witch at her side from head to toe. Ashbury had a physique with all excess chiseled away, like a blade forged to perfection. A body achieved not only through constant daily training but through devoting every aspect of one's life to the cause.

"Actually, that phrasing's off the mark. Real construction begins *before* birth... My body was *designed* for this, from the flesh to the etheric body. Generation after generation of selective breeding."

Birth was too late. Mages had always seen children as a means to achieve goals a single lifetime could not hope to realize. Ashbury's origins lay long before her conception, at the moment such sorcery began.

"Children from mage households often have their goals decided for them. In my case, that goal is to be the fastest broomrider. If I cannot achieve that goal, my entire life is forfeit."

"...Forfeit," Nanao echoed.

The girl born to fly let out a long sigh, one tinged with the bitterness of self-reproach.

"And yet, I spent too much time playing at war."

Her eyes were on the sky above, where her teammates were swinging clubs around. Their battles vicious yet delightful. Felled or feller, all took pleasure in the outcome.

That was the essence of a broom war. It was a brief respite from the pressures and duties that weighed on every mage. That was why the rules and equipment were minimal, and the players were allowed to fly free. It was little more than an extension of games children played with sticks. However high the craft involved, that essence remained. No one wished to change it.

Sensing Nanao's eyes upon her, Ashbury glanced her way.

"Look...I'm not knocking broom wars. I'm just...conscious of my own priorities."

"Mm, understood. Is there a reason you struggle to improve?"

Nanao's eyes bored right through her. Ashbury pouted.

"...You don't even hesitate to ask? I suppose that's a strength."

If anyone else had asked, she'd have dismissed the very notion. But this girl alone had no trace of ridicule, no hidden motivations. Flying with her had made that very clear.

And if she couldn't dismiss the question, then it deserved an answer. Giving up the struggle, Ashbury sighed.

"...I used to have a catcher of my own."

If you compare extraordinary talent to top-class liquor, then "barrels" capable of containing that talent are equally rare.

"...Hmph."

That was the challenge facing Ashbury on her admission to Kimberly. She soon found herself struggling to be a part of the team.

Every broomriding team had wanted her. She'd chosen the Blue

Swallows because they placed the strongest emphasis on individual skill. Given her own personality, the choice made sense—and yet, she still failed to fit in.

She was alone on the practice field. The cold night sky above only drove that fact home.

"Now, now, hold up. No one's here yet. You gonna fly without a catcher?"

Ashbury was already on her broom when a voice boomed out behind her. Surprised that anyone else was here, she turned to find a big, burly man—so oversize, he made the broom in his hand look tiny by comparison.

"Who are you?"

"Good question!" he said, as if in jest. "I'm a second-year—and I believe I'm on the same team as you."

Ashbury frowned—and then remembered.

"...Right, there was a ridiculously huge guy at the back. You were clearly in the wrong room, so I just forgot you were even there. That's hardly a body built for broomsports."

"None of us is built like *you*. But don't you frown at me—I was only ever trying to be a catcher. That's why I'm *here*."

The man flashed her a grin, and she snorted.

"I'll have you in tears by day three. You're the eighth wannabe catcher I've had! If you're just gonna shuffle uselessly around under me, I'm better off not having one."

"Lots of faith lost there, I see! But don't you worry; I ain't gonna run around like a chicken with my head cut off. I've been watching how you fly. I only need to be under you when you fall."

His confidence was blistering. He sounded like he already knew every wrinkle she could offer, and Ashbury resented that.

"You're all talk," she told him with a harsh glare. "But sure, let's see if you can back it up. You take on a five-hour practice with me, you'll soon know better."

"Afraid I've only got two hours for you. I have plans of my own!"

"Huh? Like what?"

"Barbecue party with the Labyrinth Gourmet Club. They always have the best meat!"

He flashed her a grin so bright, she shot straight past resentment and into frothing rage.

"So those animals matter more than backing me up? You've got a lot of nerve."

"Gah-ha-ha! Simmer down—you have my undivided attention for two whole hours. No matter how bad you fall, I'll be there for you. Screw up all you like!"

He just kept on winding her up. Ashbury tore her eyes off his aggravating smile, rocketing skyward and swearing the first blunder he made, she'd kick his teeth in and ban him from the practice ground without ever learning his name.

But after two hours of practice, his name was on her lips.

Those who know little of broomsports often scoff at the idea that the catcher role requires finely honed technique or compatibility with the rider. In their minds, catchers are scattered across every inch of the field, using spells to catch anyone who happens to fall their way.

Naturally, this is transparently false. If you tried covering the field in catchers so brainless they were capable only of catching people who fell their way, you'd need more than a hundred of them. But there were actually thirteen. And naturally, each was covering a *wide* range of ground.

"Tch!"

"Whew!"

Ashbury's club swung in from the side, and the opposing player dodged by the skin of his teeth. When she clucked her tongue, her prey roared back.

"That was close! But I'm not going down that easily!"

"*Hahhh—*"

And that just made her hell-bent on downing him *this* time. Her eyes never left her foe. His dodge had sent him shooting toward the ground, so she turned the tip of her broom down. As he skimmed the surface, pulling up—she was right on top, swinging down.

"...Huh? Ah, wai—!"

Her opponent saw her a moment too late. A fast swing from above—with the ground inches below. That could mean only *one* thing.

"Aughhhhh!"

And the instant her club downed her foe—before her lay an unavoidable obstacle. The ground itself, leaving her no room to maneuver.

"*Hahhhhhhh!*"

The tip of her broom brushed the grass. As it did, she yanked up hard, skimming the surface, the wind shaking the grass in her wake. The sheer force of the maneuver scrambled her guts, and her broom bucked, barely under her control. She forced all that aside, trying to ascend again.

"_____!"

But then it all caught up with her. Pulling up on the tip had lowered the base of the broom, and it caught a bump on the ground. She'd barely been maintaining her balance, and this was a fatal blow; she tried to compensate with a forward lean, but that just sent her into a vertical spin. No longer in any position to catch herself, the ground came at her—

"Elletardus! You're good."

Morgan had been waiting right in her path, a spell and his burly arms there to catch Ashbury.

"You never defy my predictions. Absolutely classic too-deep pursuit, there."

"...Can it, asshole."

Held tight in his arms, she spat venom and punched his chest. Her catcher didn't even flinch; he just flashed his pearly whites.

*   *   *

"It kills me to admit it. I couldn't for a long time," Ashbury said, pulling her gaze from the past back to the present. Looking her own weakness in the face was akin to poking a finger in an open wound. "But since he disappeared, I've been afraid to go all out. I can feel the brakes inside me as I hit the higher speeds. I don't *want* to go beyond... And ugh, I just can't *stand* that."

Ashbury's hands mussed her hair in irritation.

Watching her closely, Nanao said, "...You can't ask him to come back?"

"He went down to the labyrinth two years ago. Hasn't been seen since. Given what he was researching, odds are he was consumed by the spell a while back. Bet we'll see his coffin in the joint funeral next year."

Nanao said nothing. That was how Kimberly operated. She'd learned that truth her first year here.

"Even if he is alive—no way I'm putting my life in his hands again."

She snorted once and said nothing more. A silence settled over them. Eventually Ashbury broke it.

"...I've talked too much. Don't just listen—share something of your own. What lies ahead of you?"

"My path in life?"

"Yeah. If you wanna live by the broom, you'd better set your goals early. Try to make it as a pro broomsport athlete or be an ace flier in aerial combat—you'd shine in either role. Only difference is you're either downing people or beasts."

The moment the focus shifted away from herself, Ashbury's lips loosened. She prattled on about which pro teams would fit, how strong the player base was, which coaches she liked or couldn't stand...

A ton of specialized knowledge. All presented as options for Nanao's future—yet, to the samurai's ears, it sounded like someone else's life.

Nothing that far off felt real. She could manage a few days ahead—but Nanao still struggled to picture the distant future.

"Talk to Dustin, if you're curious. He'll be more than happy to help. He's been itching to step in; I can tell."

Ashbury had an idea what was going through Nanao's head but grinned at her anyway. Nanao nodded, appreciating less the specific advice than the kindness the older girl had shown.

After classes that same day, the usual six friends gathered in the Fellowship for dinner.

Mid-meal, Guy paused his fork. "Been meaning to ask, Nanao," he began, glancing across the table.

"Mm?" Nanao said, not used to this gravity from Guy. "Something on your mind, Guy?"

"Kinda, yeah. What's up with Ashbury? You know, the Blue Swallows' ace. You and her went at it your first match, but she hasn't been playing much lately."

In Nanao's mind, Ashbury wasn't nearly such a distant memory, having talked with her just hours before.

"I spoke to her this very morn," Nanao said. "She's distanced herself from broom wars, devoting herself to speed training."

"Oh, going for time attack? How's that working out?" Guy pressed for more information.

But the samurai just crossed her arms, eyes downcast.

"A rare sight," Chela cut in, surprised. "Nanao at a loss for words."

"Hrm. 'Tis less that I know not what to say but how much I should."

She was silenced by discretion and decorum. The Blue Swallows' ace did not often confide in others—and that knowledge made Nanao reluctant to relay their conversation. Nanao was magnificently candid, but she knew where to draw the line.

And that meant Guy couldn't exactly pry any further. Seeing their interaction at a standstill, Pete offered a helping hand.

"...He's not asking out of idle curiosity. Guy, Katie—we should share our side of things."

Pete glanced at both of them in turn and got nods back. With that, he launched into an explanation.

He started with the magical beasts attacking them on the labyrinth's second layer and how Guy had fallen off the irminsul. How an upperclassman named Morgan had stepped in to save him.

Oliver had kept silent this whole time, but his surprise was clear.

"Sounds like you had quite an adventure."

"Yeah, I know. I suck. But this guy was asking about the Blue Swallows' ace. He kinda saved my life and all, so I figured I should see what was up. He said he still swings by the second layer on the regular, so I'd like to give him an Ashbury update if I run into him again."

"Please do!" Nanao said, leaning across the table. Everyone stared at her, surprised. She looked grave. "Ashbury spoke to me about her old catcher. I imagine the man you met was one and the same. If he still lives, then I should like to reunite them."

Nanao spoke with passion, but Guy folded his arms, frowning. He remembered what *else* Morgan had said.

"I'm actually not gonna get better. Don't have much time left."

"This inferno's a real ravager. Gah-ha! I was pretty sure I could control it, but no such luck."

"I agree, but like we said, Morgan can't leave the labyrinth. Easier said than done."

He turned to Oliver and Chela, hoping their knowledge could offer a solution.

They exchanged glances and took turns replying.

"No use in us worrying about the particulars. We should start by telling each of them the facts."

"Precisely. Nanao, you talk to Ashbury. As for Morgan—Guy, Katie, Pete. If any of you find him again, fill him in."

"Will do."

"We owe him for saving Guy!"

"Always meant to."

All three nodded. But Oliver had a different concern.

"Glad to hear it," he said. "Are you sure you guys can handle the second layer, though?"

All three smiles froze. Katie and Pete both stared at their hands, their voices getting much smaller.

"…We still haven't made it over the irminsul…"

"…We got as far as the eighth marker. We're practically almost there."

"Don't forget the descent, Pete. But, uh, I think we'll manage it sometime in February."

"You can say that again! That giant tree is a huge hassle."

This last voice was far less familiar. Surprised, everyone turned toward it and found the new transfer student—Yuri Leik—grinning back at them.

Oliver narrowed his eyes, making his suspicion evident. "If you wish to join a conversation, Mr. Leik, manners dictate you say so first."

"Please, call me Yuri! And my bad—I caught ear of labyrinth chatter and couldn't stop myself. I recently got roughed up by the second layer, as it so happens! See?"

He held up his left arm and the cast on it. An unusual treatment for a mage's injury—Oliver raised an eyebrow.

"A broken arm wouldn't leave you in one of those," he said. "Was it torn off?"

"You betcha! Bird wyvern beaks are *sharp*. I've gotta keep this thing on for the next three days. It's really cramping my style!"

"You're already going that deep? Didn't you *just* get here?" Chela asked.

"Everyone said it was reckless! But it sounded like such fun, I couldn't stay away! I'll be right back in when this arm heals up."

Yuri was clearly not letting this get him down. But at this juncture, he lowered his voice and shot them a meaningful look.

"Still, it *is* a little nerve-racking on my own. Wish I had some friends to accompany me. I mean that."

"Absolutely not."

"You're a long way from *that*, Mr. Leik."

Oliver and Chela spoke on top of each other, and Yuri staggered backward as if he'd been hit by a truck.

"Harsh! But fair enough. See you in the depths! Later!"

He didn't press his luck. Yuri beat a retreat, waving his bandaged arm. Pretty sure that wasn't good for the severed limb, Oliver glanced at the next table over.

"Rossi, what do you make of him?"

"…I 'ave nothing to do with any of this. Why drag me into things, eh?" The Ytallian-accented boy had been swirling pasta around his fork.

"You two made an equally shady first impression," Oliver said.

"And *you* 'ave grown far too inclined to speak your mind!"

Despite his grumbling, Rossi turned toward them. He kept an eye on Yuri's back as the transfer student left the Fellowship.

"I 'ate to disappoint," Rossi said, snorting. "But your catch-a-thief strategy will get you nowhere. Even I find 'im sinister."

"…Specifically?" Chela asked.

Rossi put his fingers to one of his eyelids, pulling his eye wide open. "'is eyes, they are unsettling. Like a child peering into an ant 'ill."

He frowned after the departing stranger.

"I 'ave a feeling I could punch 'im in the nose, and 'is smile would not waver. And I find that honestly unnerving."

Having said his piece, Rossi turned back to his meal. Oliver frowned, chin in hand.

"…Helpful. Appreciate it, Rossi."

"You're welcome. Just remember we 'ave an appointment at seven two days 'ence."

"I'll be there," Oliver said, turning back to his own table.

Guy leaned in, whispering, "...Making a new friend?"

"Well...you fight a man once a week, you start to find some common ground."

"...Mm, I envy that," Nanao said, pursing her lips. She would love to spar with Oliver as Rossi was, but the risks were too great.

Chela gave her a pat on the back—and then yet another outside voice broke in.

"Oh, there you are. Everyone's here! Mind if I join you?"

"Er, Ms. Miligan?"

A witch with hair obscuring one eye was approaching their table. Vera Miligan.

Katie blinked in surprise, but Chela was already pulling up a chair.

"Please have a seat. We don't often see you in the Fellowship."

"Thanks. I've found a reason to ensure I'm better known around the campus."

"What reason?" Katie asked, picking up on the loaded phrasing.

Seeing the curious looks on the six friends' faces, Miligan took a sip of the tea Chela had handed her and nodded.

"Let me start from the top," she said. "Everyone's buzzing about the missing teachers, but let's not forget the more pressing issue for the students here. Anyone know what I mean?"

Katie, Guy, Pete, and Nanao all looked lost. The remaining two caught her drift and frowned.

"That's right, Oliver, Chela," Miligan said. She grinned. "It's time for—"

"We've gotta settle the problem of Godfrey's successor."

Meanwhile, behind a door emblazoned with the imposing words Campus Watch Headquarters, the current members of the Kimberly Student Council were in session.

All sides of the square table were filled up. From veteran upperclassmen to fresh recruits, from frontline fighters to behind-the-scenes support—everyone was here. And that showed how important this decision was.

The speaker sat to the left of the president's seat, a sign of her own status here. A sixth-year girl named Lesedi Ingwe.

"Those of us in the sixth year will be graduating next year. Given the time needed for the handover, we've got less than a year left. Eager beavers will already be campaigning."

"...Which means we need to choose who to back."

Alvin Godfrey sat between his two closest comrades. Purgatory himself, the current student body president. He had a grim look on his face, his hands folded—and the mood in the room was equally downbeat.

"Why the long faces?!" said a cheery voice to his right. "I'm the obvious choice!"

"Shut it, toxic gasser!" Lesedi roared, punching the table. "We've got long faces 'cause we know we can't run you!"

The blond fifth-year at Godfrey's right—Tim Linton—looked rather surprised.

"...Tim," Godfrey said reluctantly. "I appreciate your desire to succeed me. Really, I do—"

"Don't mince words, Godfrey! Give it to him straight. Nobody likes the little shit!"

Lesedi took her own advice, and there was a murmur of agreement from the room.

"It's just, everyone has their fortes, Tim," Godfrey added.

"And everyone remembers the time you poisoned the entire Fellowship," Lesedi growled. "If it weren't for that incident, we *might* have a chance of pushing you through, but..."

Every member present nodded, wincing. Trying to shake off the mood, an older student clapped their hands.

"But hey, that's in the past. No use yelling at Tim *now*. We'll just have to find a decent candidate from the fourth- or fifth-years. Not me, though."

"Or me…"

"Honestly, I don't think I even could."

Half the members present—primarily back-line members—quickly ruled themselves out. Predictable but nonetheless cause for Lesedi's headache.

"…Please, people. We're not saying you need to be Purgatory II. Just keep the Campus Watch going as the new president—"

"Yeah, but that's the thing."

"We *will* be compared. Constantly."

"Kimberly isn't exactly peaceful as it is."

"You need substantial might. You've gotta be in the top third of the upperclassmen, at least."

An accurate analysis. As much as Lesedi wanted to argue otherwise, she and Godfrey knew better. Everyone bowing out was not doing so out of fear but from a rational assessment of their own prowess.

Still, that wasn't *everyone*. A few hands went up—about half the remaining members.

"…I really don't think I'm meant for it, but if there's nobody else…I could try?"

"Same here. Godfrey got things moving in the right direction. I don't want to see that fizzle out."

"…Me neither!"

Godfrey looked the volunteers over, smiling.

"Thanks. We appreciate it," he said.

"Hmm… I figured as much, but they're all front liners," Lesedi muttered. She was stroking her chin.

All the volunteers had served on the Watch's vanguard. They'd been through one battle after another. Absolutely worth relying on in a fight—but their strengths leaned hard that way. Not many of them had a mind for politics. Godfrey himself had never been a political mastermind but had the charisma and leadership skills to make up for that.

"They're better than Tim, but none of these options is exactly a sure thing. Let's change tactics. Who are we expecting to run who isn't part of the current council?"

Sensing they were at an impasse, Lesedi turned to other matters. A girl across from her pulled out some documents: a list with several student names.

"It goes without saying, but the former student council faction will be nominating several candidates. They're really gunning for it."

"Of course they are," Godfrey said with a nod. "They've been out of power for three years and want it back."

Wincing at the tension, the student with the list looked for better news. "Um, but there are candidates with positions closer to ours. Especially viable ones include—"

"—Vera Miligan, next student body president. Has a ring to it, yes?"

The Snake-Eyed Witch flashed an intrepid grin. All eyes widened.

"...Um, you mean...?"

"You're gonna run?"

"Yes. I thought it might be interesting, running for Kimberly student body president on a pro–civil rights platform."

Miligan took another sip of tea. Oliver and Chela fell silent, considering her plan.

"...If the Godfrey camp doesn't have a clear successor, the election could be a real free-for-all."

"And you mean to take advantage of that? Teaming up with the current council?"

"I knew you two would get it. Exactly. With the current spread, the votes could well swing my way."

Oliver nodded. Without an obvious candidate, elections might end up snatched away by a dark horse. Kimberly was no exception. Miligan was likely one of several candidates making a similar play.

"That said, I'm not hell-bent on winning no matter the cost. It's more that I don't want the current student council displaced. I rather like Kimberly as it is and am loath to see it revert to pre-Godfrey days."

"…Was it that bad?"

"Mm. In case you weren't aware, the Kimberly elections give the student body president the power to assemble a council. Who is assigned to what role is entirely up to that president, so a single election could well replace *everybody*. As Godfrey himself did when he founded the Campus Watch," Miligan explained. "I've known the current core members since they took over, ever since they were simply a neighborhood watch with no real authority. You can imagine why I'd want to have their backs now."

Miligan was looking for sympathy. It might not be a complete fabrication, but none of the six friends was dumb enough to think that was her *real* reason for running. She definitely had goals of her own. The question was—what did that mean to them?

Katie had suffered more than any of them at Miligan's hands. There was a long, weighty silence, an internal struggle like holding your face in a basin of cold water, and at last Katie croaked out her answer.

"……………You have…my support."

"Thank you, Katie. I hoped you would say that."

Miligan reached out both hands, tenderly rumpling that curly hair. Then she turned her eyes to the others.

"If the need arises, I can redirect my votes to the current student council's candidate. Depending on how the election is going, I may end up having their votes flow to me. That's how alliances work."

Oliver knew this was true. From what he'd heard, Miligan was currently expecting nothing more than a decent shot if the election turned her way. She didn't see herself as any more viable than the other candidates. And that meant she was unlikely to be *too* caught up in winning. There were substantial benefits to having whoever *was* elected owe you.

But while Oliver considered her motives carefully, Guy raised a hand.

"Question for ya."

"Naturally. Ask anything you'd like, Guy."

"Gotcha. The election's next year, so anyone chosen would take over then. But you'd be a sixth-year, so even if you're elected president, your term would end the year after when you graduate. Does that mean there'd be another election?"

"Ah, I see. A technical question. Basically, no, there wouldn't be. The presidential term is a hard three years. If the president graduates during that time, they name a successor at will, who serves out the remainder of the president's term. Which means anyone from the fourth- through sixth-years can run. Seventh-years *are* disqualified, though."

"Okay, that makes sense. So you'd graduate halfway through your term, but anyone you choose could take over."

"In theory, yes...but I'd likely find myself beholden to the opinions of others. Even if I do manage to claim the presidency, Godfrey's faction would be heavily involved. At best, I could make a strong push for a successor. Katie, what say you? You'd be a fifth-year by the time I graduate."

"Stop! My head's about to explode! I can't afford to think about anything else right now!"

Katie had both hands over her ears. Miligan smiled at her and turned back to the others once more.

"I believe I do have *some* measure of popularity. Whether I'm elected or not, I have no intention of being a mere fringe candidate. Once I commit, I'm all in," Miligan told them. "And that's where you come in. Your group stands out from the underclassman crowd, and your voices will influence the decisions of students in your year or below. I'm not asking for anything outrageous, simply that you make it public knowledge that Vera Miligan has your vote. That alone could turn the tide."

Her position made clear, she now sought direct support. Everyone exchanged glances.

"I won't force you into it," Miligan added. "I'm sure Godfrey has helped you all, and if there's someone from the current council camp you'd like to back, do so. Just remember what I've said: A vote for me counts as a vote for them. Bear that in mind."

And with that, the Snake-Eyed Witch rose to her feet.

"That's my piece. Now I'm going to make the rounds and ensure some more kids know who I am."

Miligan turned and left the table. The group watched her go, and eventually, Pete broke the silence.

"…I'm gonna vote for her. There's nobody else I'm particularly enthused about. And given what she did for us during the Salvadori incident…I can't really blow her off."

"I didn't even get to tag along then…so I guess I'm in the same position," Guy said.

"I see no reason to refuse," Nanao proclaimed. "Ms. Miligan has my vote as well."

Chela took note of all this and considered the matter. "…It's hard to just forget about her kidnapping Katie. But she has done a lot to make up for it. And Katie herself has put it behind her. Still…I think I want to see how the field is stacking up before making a decision."

Her eyes turned toward Oliver.

He thought a moment longer, then spoke with caution. "…Same here. There's a few things I'd like to check on first."

Their choices here could transform the school, and he wasn't in a position to make that decision lightly. Chela nodded her agreement and reached for her now-cold tea.

"…But if the election's going to be a free-for-all, I'm curious who else will throw their hats in."

*　　*　　*

Like Miligan had explained, elections at Kimberly chose a single president—and that president picked the council. No matter the role, the people chosen would all be from that candidate's faction.

Naturally, that meant nobody ran for the office without some level of support. The vast majority of candidates had a sizable crowd of supporters—and once elected, that crowd would become the new council. Godfrey had pulled members of his old neighborhood watch—Tim Linton, Lesedi Ingwe, and the late Carlos Whitrow. All people who'd been with him from the start.

But the opposite was equally true. Groups gave rise to connections, and even if they lost control of the council itself, the ties among members were not easily lost. In other words—those students involved with the *previous* student council were still around. And they were looking for a comeback.

The labyrinth's first layer—the quiet, wandering path. A layer packed with unofficial meeting spots for students of all ages. The comforting, polished sound of a shaker filled one of these secret rooms.

"...And done," a slender man said, pouring the cocktail into three glasses. "A toast to the start of war—is it too early to celebrate our victory?"

He threw the very full glasses across the room like darts. The drinks spun through the air, spilling not a drop, landing neatly in the hands of their targets.

"We've spent years planning for this," said a woman leaning against the wall. "Nothing but total victory is even worth considering."

She had pale skin, even by the standards of Yelgland natives. Coupled with her long, pointed ears, she was unmistakably an elf.

The slender man set the shaker down, raising a brow. "I thought three years were but the passing of the wind to your kind."

"I'm *impatient*. That's why I left the forest. Don't make me say it again, Barman."

The elf grinned and knocked back the contents of her glass. She licked her lips, savoring the burning of the liquor in her throat and letting it intoxicate her, then conquering that feeling. Students with a taste for spirits had deemed the Barman's work worth ten thousand belc a glass for good reason.

"Watch me trample all competition," a fussy-looking male said. "Not only Godfrey's would-be heir but all the other bric-a-brac."

He set his drink down untouched, kneeling before the upperclassman seated at the back of the room. The man so honored nodded quietly, his long blond hair swaying. He was tall, with strong, handsome features, and half his face was covered with red scars from an old burn. His once-flawless visage now held an unsettling intensity.

"Make it so. This shall be the final year this campus lies in Purgatory's hands," the blond man said. "We shall declare your candidacy. And with it, the restoration of the old ways. Let all voices cry out—we alone are fit to be the Kimberly Student Council!"

The man's scarred beauty twisted as he spoke. His name—Leoncio Echevalria. Alvin Godfrey's primary opponent in the previous election.

"You want to see Noll spitting blood, writhing in agony?"

A stabbing pain in her chest. Gwyn's words echoed through her mind, forcing her to confront her own shortcomings.

"There is nothing you can do here."

That much, she'd known from the start. Everything seemed to remind her of that fact—of how the lord she'd sworn to protect with her life fought against the old man, burning himself as fuel.

She could still see it: inexhaustible admiration for his late mother paired with self-loathing for how little he resembled her. Those volatile emotions clawing their way out of him. How could so much adoration, pain, conflict, and consternation fit inside one boy?

She'd fallen into a trance, unable to tear her eyes away. Once the machine god appeared and the soul merge began, there wasn't a single thing a covert operative could do. And that realization made her feel like a feeble, worthless puppet.

She wished to ease his pain.

To heal his suffering.

To be far, far closer to his heart.

Yet, the means to that eluded her. Hide, peek, and ambush. Her role had taught her those skills and nothing more. She'd learned that nothing else was needed, that everything else must be left behind.

And that left her wanting to say something to him, but she was unable to find the words.

"—sa? Um, Teresa?"

In a lounge filled with chattering underclassmen, a girl was worrying about her friend.

Teresa had been staring fixedly at space, not moving a muscle. Rita Appleton was watching her carefully, fretting. When Teresa still failed to respond, the boy in the seat across from her—Dean—slapped the table.

"Hey! Rita's talking to you!" he snarled.

At last, Teresa's eyes snapped into focus. She gave Dean a look like one might regard a pebble in one's path and then turned to Rita.

"…I didn't notice. Did you need something?"

"N-not *need*, really, but…you're being *extra* quiet. Is something wrong?"

Rita appeared scared to even ask, but Teresa just looked away.

"Not really. And if there was, I wouldn't talk to any of you about it."

Without thinking, she reached for the cup in front of her and took a sip. When she tried to swallow, her throat spasmed, and she spat tea everywhere.

"T-Teresa?!" Rita yelped.

"Finally gotcha!" Dean cried, pumping a fist.

Teresa spluttered a few moments longer, then looked up, her lips red and swollen.

"…What is this?" she asked.

"Tea. With a secret ingredient."

Dean dangled a little vial by the side of his head. Inside was essence of angry radish. As delighted as he was by the success of the prank, his smile faded fast.

"You'd normally see right through a trick like this. But today, you straight-up chugged it. That's not like you at all. Your mind must be somewhere else entirely."

"I don't…know what you mean. Do you have a death wish?"

There was undeniable hostility in her eyes. When he saw that, Peter Cornish quickly poked his friend in his side.

"D-Dean! You'd better say sorr—"

"Hell no. I finally got one in."

Not only was Dean not backing down, he got up and moved right into Teresa's face. There was a lot of pent-up anger and frustration involved, and neither Rita nor Peter dared intervene.

"Take a hint," Dean said. "Ever since you mocked me in our first class, I've been trying to start this fight."

"……"

"I don't care if you think less of me. That pisses me off, but I know full well I'm totally outclassed here. What I can't stand is how you don't even *notice* us. Not me, not Peter, and not even Rita, no matter how much she looks after you."

He ground his teeth together—then spun on his heel, tossing the next words over his shoulder.

"I ain't one to stand around bitching. Neither are you! Let's take this outside."

"......"

He stalked off, and a few moments later, Teresa shot out of her seat, heading after him. Rita and Peter trailed behind.

By the time the four of them reached the gardens outside, quite a crowd had picked up on the front pair's scowls. It was clear at a glance where *this* was heading, and an audience was gathering.

"Oh, first-years fighting?"

"A duel, huh? I'll ref it!"

To the older students, this was less a spectacle than an obligation. The upperclassmen had stepped in to watch over their fights, and they were doing the same. A school tradition passed down through the years.

Out on the grass, Dean turned to face Teresa, muttering, "Seriously, nobody's coming to stop us? That's Kimberly for you."

He was half impressed and half appalled. But that thought soon faded away. He drew his athame, pointing the sharp end at her. Teresa blinked, then belatedly drew her own. Both chanted a dulling spell. If they skipped that part, the older kids would *definitely* intervene.

"Y-you don't have to…!" Rita warbled, unable to bear it.

Peter just put a hand on her shoulder. "Watch closely. Once Dean gets like this, there's no stopping him."

"But…!"

"I figured he and Teresa would go at it eventually."

She hadn't expected Peter to take this in stride. And he had a point—Rita had certainly been well aware of the friction between her two friends. She'd also been worried it would explode one day. Still...

"But...Dean can't win," Rita whispered.

She'd gone so far as to envision the fight's outcome.

"Maybe not," Peter said, looking tense. "Still, though...I have faith in him."

His voice didn't waver. This faith was earned. And as they watched, Dean finished casting the dulling spell, raised his left hand, and punched himself in the nose.

"Er...?!"

"Don't worry. That's how he does it."

Peter made that sound reassuring. Dean was letting blood drip from his nose onto the grass at his feet.

"Nosebleeds clear his head."

As if proving that, the stance he struck was legitimate. A Lanoff high stance with clear indications he'd originally been self-taught.

"I'm ready," he said, his voice calm. "You?"

"...Anytime."

Teresa was barely in a stance at all. She didn't rate her opponent high enough to even *bother*. And Dean's athame shot out, trying to overturn that dismissal.

"*Huff...!*"

There was a quiet *tink* as Teresa's blade deflected it. They'd started at one-step, one-spell distance. Neither had made any prior demands on the rules, so it defaulted to all-inclusive—incantations allowed. But neither seemed inclined to step back to *that* range for the simple reason that neither wanted to be the first to back down.

"*...Haaah...!*"

Yet, Dean's bladework showed an eerie calm. He wasn't letting his temper get the best of him and lunging too far in or being too tentative; he was keeping up the pressure from above, watching for an opening. Teresa was fending him off without difficulty but also not taking the offense herself. The crowd hadn't expected such a quiet duel between two first-years, and they began discussing it among themselves.

"Hmm, they've both got moves."

"The boy's swings are a bit too wild still."

"Snap decisions, bold when they need to be."

"The girl's far more skilled, but her heart's not in it."

Ten ripostes in, and anyone with a good eye would have a read on the duelists. Rita looked genuinely surprised.

"Since when can Dean fight like this?"

This was heartfelt. She'd been convinced Teresa would down him in seconds. Teresa was definitely being unusually passive, which worked in Dean's favor, but Dean's own skills left Rita wide-eyed. He was like a totally different person from the hothead she knew.

"...Rita, have you heard of the Warren Peak Tragedy? It's been five years now, but..."

Rita hadn't expected Peter to bring *that* up in the middle of a fight. She blinked at him. But the name sounded familiar, and she soon dug up the memory.

"...I do. It was in the papers. A wild griffin snatched a bunch of children from a village, and several perished before it was taken down."

"Yeah. Nineteen kids were taken. The griffin killed and ate seventeen of them."

Peter's voice was grim. That was a tragic end, even by animal-attack standards. And just as Rita was starting to wonder how this was relevant...

"The two survivors...were me, and Dean."

She stopped breathing. In front of her, the fighters hit their twentieth exchange, neither finding a decisive opening, both still locked in the one-step, one-spell range.

"You really are *way* off your game. I can *feel* it."

Dean's voice was a low growl. He'd known the gap in their abilities from the start. The bloodletting had cleared his mind, and he was fighting passably, but there were also things he could see *because* he was calm. For instance—how she could have cut his head off ten times by now if she felt like it.

"What's eating you, anyway? Does it really matter more than kicking my ass?"

"……"

Teresa wasn't talking, wasn't letting her face show any emotion, but inside, she was completely at a loss. She couldn't make up her mind what outcome she was even hoping for.

She had chances to get her blade to his throat or pierce above his heart with the tip. But she worried if she went for those, she'd betray the assassin training drilled into her. She had to fend off Dean Travers within the parameters of a first-year's skill, in a fair fight. And those constraints meant less than a tenth of her real abilities were on offer.

On top of that, there was the question of her own motivation. If simply winning would satisfy her, she'd have done it already. But that wasn't it. This irritation wasn't going anywhere, even if she shucked off the dulling spell and chopped his head off. She had no clue how to *release* this emotion, and because of that…

"Okay, lemme guess. I bet…it's that older boy you dote on. Did he turn on ya? Was he all like, *You're such a downer! Never show your face here again!*"

The upshot: For a second, she forgot her worries.

She stopped thinking. She balled her left fist and slammed it into his chin.

"Gah…!"

The blow caught him by surprise, and he reeled backward. Teresa followed it with a toe kick to his abdomen, and when he fell to his knees, she flung herself at him. As the audience gaped, her athame went flying, and she unleashed a barrage of blows to his face.

"Oh… Ohhh…!"

Dean did his best to ward them off, using his arms as a shield, watching her through the gap. He had *never* seen her look like this. Rage and frustration, shame and disappointment, all crumpled up and mixed together. Like she was shouting something, like she was about to burst into tears—her expressionless mask was completely gone. This was the face of an actual *person*.

"…Ha-ha. See, you *can* do emotions!"

Even as she hit him again, he found himself grinning. *This* was what he'd been after. It all made sense. So he dropped his own athame and punched her right back. Blood started gushing from her nose.

This was no longer a duel. No techniques or skills involved. Just a children's brawl, both swinging fists fueled by rage and tenacity. The fistfight lasted a good five minutes, ending when yet another blow to his chin finally knocked Dean down. Teresa jumped right on top of him, trying to hit him more, but that was when the ref stepped in and pinned her arms behind her back.

"Okay, okay, that's enough! The girl wins!"

"Um, hmm. The back half was a total shit show."

"Ha-ha! C'mon, it was very *first-year*."

With the fight over, the crowd began to shuffle off. The ref was gradually talking Teresa down, and her head got level enough to take in the scene. Dean was on the ground, his face swollen up—and judging by how Teresa's eyes barely opened, she likely wasn't in any better shape. Meanwhile, off to the side—their other two friends appeared to be at a loss for words.

"…Teresa…," Rita managed, cautiously approaching her friend. Teresa instantly turned tail and fled, gone before anyone could say another word.

"And there she goes… Uh, Dean, you alive?"

"…Ugh…gah…"

There was a faint groan from the ground. Peter winced and knelt down.

"Yeah, that chin's broken. Better get you to the infirmary. Rita, help me carry him."

"Uh, okay…"

Rita hustled over, and they each got a shoulder under his arms, staggering off toward the school building.

That evening, Oliver was on the first layer of the labyrinth, quietly heading toward his cousins' lair. The stony paths changed on a daily basis, but he'd been making this trip long enough to recognize the patterns. Choosing branches that would help him avoid traps, beasts, and other students, he could now make smooth, steady progress.

Twenty minutes in, he stopped.

"I know you're there, Ms. Carste," he called out.

His voice echoed through the hall, returning only silence. He waited, not moving.

"…If you don't want to show yourself, I won't insist."

He sighed and took a step forward. The air behind him rippled.

"…I'm here."

Oliver turned to find his covert operative kneeling at his feet. Her head was much further down than usual, preventing him from seeing her face. He could imagine why.

"Look at me."

"……"

If her lord ordered it, Teresa could not refuse. She reluctantly lifted her head. Her cheeks, forehead, and eyes—every part of her face was covered in painful bruises.

"Quite a beating," Oliver said, grimacing. "That's all from Mr. Travers, I assume?"

As he spoke, he gently ran his fingers down her cheek. Teresa had clearly done her best to patch it up. With her healing skills, however, it would take more than a few hours to eliminate that kind of swelling. Skilled healers could leave no trace at all, but this girl hadn't been trained for that.

"I'm aware you were fighting with your hands tied, but even so… your classmates are better than you thought, right?"

He spoke softly, drawing his white wand and bringing it to her face. He chanted a spell and carefully eliminated the injuries, leaving no detail untouched. Teresa silently let him get to work but eventually asked, "…You're not going to reprimand me?"

She sounded confused.

"I am not. I was in far more fights my first year."

Clearly, he was still kicking himself for some of those. He gave her face one last check. This whole time, she'd kept her eyes screwed tightly shut, as if she didn't dare meet his gaze.

"But I was surprised to hear you went at it. You've always ignored the bait and walked away before. What's going on?" he asked.

This question took her a long time to answer. At last, her voice quivering, she managed, "I owe you…an apology."

"An apology…? For what?"

"When the target broke through the barrier—I failed to finish him off."

Her voice broke from the remorse. It caught Oliver unguarded, and he winced.

"Of all the— That's nothing to be ashamed of. Quite the opposite, actually. Landing a deep cut on him made *all* the difference. No one else could have done it. You should be proud."

Oliver lavished praise, but Teresa was shaking her head, rejecting it emphatically. Her feelings on that were clearly set in stone.

"If I had finished him there, we'd have lost far less."

"All of us could say the same. It's not on you."

He spoke with force this time. This had been *his* plan, and no one bore more responsibility for the outcome. He was not putting one iota of that on *her*.

"But I get why you feel that way. Eleven deaths. Eleven of us gone. Under my orders, to slay *my* enemy."

He remembered each face that had perished for his desire. The days he'd spent with them, the words they'd exchanged echoing through his mind. Oliver's hands grasped Teresa's shoulders, so grateful for her warmth that he could cry.

"And that's why it's such a relief…that you're still here."

He let that relief permeate his voice.

You being here, alive—that's what matters. Not what you did or didn't do. Only your survival.

And before his very eyes—large tears started spilling down the girl's cheeks.

"?!"

Shock took his breath away. It was as if the dams on Teresa's tear ducts had broken. Nothing in her previous behavior would have suggested this was even possible, and Oliver was at a loss.

"Wh-what's this, Ms. Carste? Why…are you crying…?"

He could not offer solace when he didn't know the cause. He listened closely, trying to ascertain the source of the girl's despair from between her sobs.

"…It's…my role to…serve you. But I…"

Her words came in fits and gasps. Pain she could not share, suffering that lay beyond her means—and that had been too much to bear.

"…I couldn't…do anything… I couldn't ease any of it… Your pain, your worries…your torment…"

From that point on, she managed nothing else with meaning, simply wailing like a lost child. Oliver found his arms around her, her body held close against his—a body so much smaller than he had imagined.

"You helped," he said. "This here—this helped, Teresa."

For the first time, he spoke her name. He'd kept her at arm's length, but that impulse vanished without a trace.

"I should have realized. When you didn't show yourself right away— this was why."

If only he'd been more perceptive. Instead, he'd overlooked the intensity of her feelings until she put them into words, allowing her to stew in this anguish.

"...Please don't let that prey on you. My pain and suffering—those are things I *earned*. All these indelible sins one on top of the other... Having you serve me is but *one* of those sins."

He did not deserve her concern. To Oliver, this girl and her role were yet another transgression. But that was merely his perspective. If the vassals staking their lives on his cause had feelings for him—

"Is there anything I can do for you?" he asked. "I would like...to make amends. To honor your efforts and feelings."

She was already in his arms, but he felt the need to inquire. He entreated her to ask something of him. Her feelings had grown without his knowledge; he had been ignorant of her suffering, and only with her tears did awareness dawn. He didn't wish for their connection to end with that.

"......h......"

"Mm?"

Her answer was lost in a sob, but his ears caught a fragment of a word. And as if atoning for his previous oversight, this time, he could sense her desire.

"...Like this?"

One hand beneath her knees, the other around her back, Oliver gently lifted her up. She was achingly light. Teresa's slender arms wrapped around his neck, pulling herself closer, her nose burying itself in his shoulder. Like a child clinging to a parent.

"Oh," he said. "You just needed a hug."

"_____!"

She pinched his shoulder in protest. He smiled and patted her back.

"Didn't mean to ruin it. Stay like that as long as you need," he said. "...Let's go for a stroll. That's what I'm in the mood for."

With Teresa in his arms, he faced front and resumed his trek. He didn't care if anyone saw them. If a child cried, you held them until they were done. No one in this world could possibly argue otherwise.

*　　*　　*

They were still like that when he reached his cousins' atelier.

"………"

"I told her to take as long as she needed. Let her have this one, Gwyn."

His brother had certainly given them a piercing glare, but he took that in stride. He carried Teresa over to his usual chair and settled into it. She didn't budge. He'd assumed she'd let go once they got here, but clearly not. Seeing the look of resignation on his face, Shannon smiled.

"That's good. Teresa…wanted this. For…a long time."

Teresa didn't respond to that, either, but her ears turned red—clearly caught between the desire to remain in this embrace and the shame of having everyone looking.

"…Is that true, Teresa?" Oliver asked, stroking her ear with one finger. She jumped and then pinched his shoulder hard. "Sorry, sorry," he said.

Then he managed to gather himself, glancing at Gwyn.

"We need to talk about the student body president. Who do we want winning?"

Given the state of the school, this was a pressing concern. Gwyn was busy working on his viola but spoke as he worked.

"It's more who do we *not* want winning."

"Namely…?"

"Under Godfrey, Kimberly has been much more favorable to our operations. Primarily because we've maintained cordial relations with his camp. But if we revert to the previous leadership, that all changes. We have comrades on their side, too…but since we've been openly supporting Godfrey for a while, I can't say we have much influence in the previous council faction."

"So we're inclined to back the Campus Watch's candidate?"

"Yes, but if that looks doomed, we'll have to push someone who leans Godfrey's way. We're planning on having a few comrades run as well. Some of them are already on the current council."

Gwyn's explanation all made sense. Oliver thought for a moment, hesitating, then asked, "...No plans to place it entirely under our control?"

He owed Godfrey and was therefore reluctant to wrest power from him, but Purgatory, too, was a lord—one with a powerful following. And if his power could be theirs, the attempt might be worth considering. That sentiment fueled the question.

"We've certainly thought about it. But it puts us in the limelight. Our strength derives from staying hidden—nobody even realizes we're such a force to be reckoned with. Slipping a few comrades in, we can do, but if we band together and run the council ourselves, there's a risk of revealing our hand. We don't want to give the faculty any leads."

A sound argument, and one that came as a relief. There was no need to betray Godfrey's kindness or strength—at least, not yet.

"And one more thing—there's an investigation underway. We expected as much, but the student body isn't exempt from the suspect list for the slain instructors."

A new topic to consider. Oliver set his mind to it. They might be backing the Godfrey camp in the election, but *this* fight was entirely their own.

"We can assume they'll place spies among the students. We won't allow them to infiltrate our comrades—but make sure you're careful about associating with anyone new."

"I always am. That said..."

Gwyn's comment had brought a shady face to Oliver's mind. From day one, that boy had been suspicious—and not a faint suspicion but a clear and obvious one.

"...is a second-year named Yuri Leik on your radar? He claimed to have transferred in from a nonmagical school."

"I've been briefed. The timing alone makes him impossible to ignore, but if he is a faculty spy, the means of injecting him is a tad *too* obvious. It could be merely coincidence—or maybe that's the *intent*. I've yet to get my head around it. We'll keep probing."

Oliver nodded. Mages residing in villages or towns often grew up with ordinaries, and it wasn't unheard of for them to enroll in a magical school later on. If they took Yuri at his word, then he was one of those. Calling that a "transfer" was less common, but it could be he was just using language common in nonmagical facilities or had simply decided "transfer" would be easier to grasp than "late enrollment."

It was all highly unusual, but Oliver also felt that if this was a ploy, the faculty would have hidden it better. Whatever the plan—or lack of one—was, Oliver and the rest would just have to watch the boy carefully.

"While we can't ignore the election itself, our priority lies elsewhere. We already have plans in place to turn the teaching staff against one another. I'll need your double for a few days."

"Theo? Go right ahead. Who are we targeting specifically?" Oliver asked.

Gwyn's next words sent a chill down his spine.

"Vanessa Aldiss. The teacher with the loosest hold on her temper."

CHAPTER 3

The Grilling

Disaster occurred during second period that morning. The first sword arts class Oliver had attended since relieving his double.

"…"

"What's the matter, Oliver? You don't look so good."

Students were finishing up their sets and moving into the skirmish phase. Oliver was staring pensively at his athame. Sensing something amiss, Chela approached, but before he could answer, Rossi chimed in.

"The 'eat is on! Oliver, will you do the honors?"

"…We've already got a duel set for tomorrow, though."

"Don't be such a stick-in-the-mud, eh? We rush straight to the main event, and you will be left astonished by my progress!"

Not waiting for an answer, Rossi pulled him toward the practice area. Oliver had no plans to turn down a sparring match—that wasn't the problem here. It all just felt so *wrong*. Unable to shake that, he found himself facing Rossi at one-step, one-spell range.

"Ready? 'Ere we go!"

Rossi was already moving. He was melding the boldness of his self-taught style with the tricky techniques of the Koutz school, and it was getting harder and harder to read his approach. Oliver couldn't afford a lapse of attention. He hit his usual Lanoff midstance, ready to parry.

"……Uh?"

They'd made it eight ripostes. Rossi let out a shocked grunt, and an athame clattered to the floor—knocked from Oliver's hand by a blow to his wrist.

"«««««««_____?!"»»»»»»»»

A moment later, students in all directions turned to stare. Rossi taking a run against Oliver was a regular feature of this class—including the outcome, which invariably involved him being outmatched and sent packing. Everyone knew how things were supposed to go. Until now. And this didn't happen at the end of a furious exchange but during the initial warm-up phase.

"......!"

Oliver was staring at his hand in shock, and his friends came running over. Guy, Katie, and Pete formed a shield in front of him and glared at Rossi.

"Rossi, you ass! I thought you were better than that!"

"I know you crave victory, but using poison?!"

"Oliver, what's wrong?! What did he do to you?!"

"My honor lies besmirched! I swear, I am innocent! Upon my word as a Ytallian!"

Rossi threw up his hands in the face of this interrogation. More students joined the fray, and the commotion got loud enough that Garland turned to address the class—but just in time, Oliver himself spoke up.

"...He's telling the truth. He did nothing untoward."

A hush settled over the crowd. Oliver collected his athame and sheathed it. Then he pushed through the students to Rossi, doing his best to smile.

"Victory is yours, Rossi. You finally got me."

He gave the Ytallian a congratulatory pat on the shoulder. Rossi was just gaping at him, and their respective reactions were making the crowd rethink things.

"...You're off your game, Mr. Horn," Stacy Cornwallis said.

Fay Willock nodded. "Are you sure there are no poison or curses involved? Those would be less shocking than this."

Across the room, Richard Andrews was giving Oliver a dubious look. And a similar thought had the room buzzing again.

"...Then..."

"…He's just having a bad day?"

"Bad enough that Rossi overcame a year of trouncing…?"

And as that notion spread, there was a *thud*.

"Any nobodies dreaming of seizing this chance, line up before me! I'll crush you all in turn."

Joseph Albright was in the center of the room, flashing his most terrifying smile. A few students had taken a step toward Oliver, but they scattered like spider hatchlings. As skirmishes started up again in all directions, Guy, Katie, and Pete turned to Rossi. The three friends looked chagrined.

"Sorry I doubted ya, Rossi."

"You really didn't poison him… I'm sorry, too."

"Same here. I just figured it was the most likely situation."

"You are all 'orrible at apologies! Argh, I cannot call this a victory."

Rossi was tearing his hair out. He heaved an especially dramatic sigh, stepped over to Oliver, and took a firm grip on his shoulder. Half disgruntled, half encouraging.

"Get your 'ead back in the game before we next meet, please. The duel is off until then."

"…Thanks," Oliver said, glad for the offer.

In lieu of further sparring, he and Chela paired off, focusing on core forms while he attempted to adjust himself. They were still at it when class ended.

After class, he'd pushed away his friends' concerns and was now walking alone down a deserted corridor.

"…Ngh…"

Oliver was shaking with fear and frustration. It had been tough to keep a lid on that in front of his friends, but he knew the real horror lay once he was alone again. There was no one else here. And that forced him to face himself.

This was not *"off his game"* or *"a slump."* Nothing that mild. This was *not his body.* Movements acquired through dizzying amounts of training no longer functioned at all. This wasn't *"something wrong."* There was no part of him that *wasn't* wrong.

And he knew why this was happening. Only too well. The soul merge—there was little doubt that that one spell cast on him during the Enrico fight was to blame for his condition. When he'd woken after three days and nights of torment, he'd noticed the problem right away. He'd hoped it was simply a by-product of his injuries and fatigue and gone about his life like normal, but those hopes had been betrayed. Beyond a shadow of a doubt.

"…Guh…"

Something vital had *broken.* That was a terrifying notion, but nonetheless, it was the first thing that came to mind.

And he could find no argument against it. It was a miracle he'd spent several minutes fused to Chloe Halford's soul and lived to tell the tale. Others could heal his wounds, but none could say how bad the damage *inside* was.

Even mages weren't capable of repairing *all* damage with a healing spell. The soul itself was the prime example, but damage to the ether or flesh could be equally irreversible. Restoration of anything related to mana circulation was extremely delicate. Growth and training created countless rivers of magic, branching and diving; the system was unique to each individual, and the shape of it was a mage's power. The etheric body and soul *remembered* that layout, so it would not be lost in a routine injury. But there were exceptions. Specifically, any time the injuries extended *beyond* the purview of the etheric body.

And if that applied here—then all the strength Oliver Horn had gleaned in life may have been lost forever, all for the sake of a few minutes' combat.

He couldn't yet know that this was true. He knew not to leap to conclusions. But his hopes felt all too feeble. He'd been helpless to defend

himself against Rossi, and that had fanned the flames of his fears. That
outcome was more eloquent than a thousand rationales.

Dark thoughts flowed through him without end. Oliver shook
his head, trying to cast them out. Whatever the truth might be,
dwelling on it here would get him nowhere. He needed to speak to
his cousins—then they could decide. He tried to force his feet into
motion…

"Come, Oliver."

…and he saw a girl's hand held out to him.

"…Nanao…?"

He raised his head and found the Azian girl before him, her smile
unwavering. He instinctively reached for her outstretched hand,
which then closed around his. The warmth flowing into him was genuinely astounding. Only then did he realize how cold he was.

"Warm, yes? My mother sang its virtues. Said with me by her side,
she needn't heat any stones all winter through."

Sharing her warmth with him, Nanao pulled Oliver along. His gaze
was glued to her back. And he remembered doing the same thing—
down darkened paths, with his own mother.

"You have nothing to fear. Nothing at all."

His eyes were wet with tears. They left a trail on the ground where
the two of them passed.

Late at night that same evening, on the edge of the labyrinth's fifth
layer—Firedrake Canyon, where the wyverns nested.

"Oh, Lu! How nice of you to drop by."

Collapsed against the sheer rock face were the remains of the
machine god, beside which stood a shadowy figure like darkness
given human form. She waved cheerily. Few shortened Luther Garland's name quite so drastically, but he nonetheless lowered his head
in reverence.

"...Thank you for keeping the scene safe, Ms. Muwezicamili."

"Awww, why so formal? We used to be thick as thieves."

Baldia Muwezicamili was the school's foremost expert on curses, but perhaps not manners. Garland deflected her claim with a faint smile, turning his eyes to the golem's remains—and the back of the old woman standing astride it.

"Have I kept you waiting long, Instructor Gilchrist?"

"A mere three minutes. A trifle. Compared to your time as a student."

Frances Gilchrist had been alive for a thousand years and teaching spellology for an equally dizzying length of time. A sarcastic dig at Garland's student days was more than enough to silence the man. Behind him, Baldia's black cloak rippled like water as she laughed.

"Lu was *always* tardy!"

"...Let's get to the point. The reason we're here—"

"Naturally, I'm concerned about the same thing. What lies on the *other side*," Gilchrist intoned, pointing her white wand at the remains.

Garland nodded, and behind him, Baldia folded her pale arms.

"It *is* the obvious thing," she said. "I'd love to turn it over, but if I try, it'll wind up all cursed. It would be so easy if we could call Vana here."

"I came before that could happen. Ms. Aldiss lacks the delicacy required and could easily destroy the evidence we seek," Gilchrist said.

With that, she leaped off the machine god to the ground below. Well aware of his role here, Garland stepped alongside, raising his own wand.

"And I'm your backup? Fair enough. Flipping this mass is a tall order, but between the two of us—"

"Don't be daft. I called you to bear witness to the accuracy of the evidence."

She pushed her former student's wand out of the way, then gently waved her own, chanting a spell.

"Revolve inversum."

And her incantation lifted the entire bulk into the air without so much as a single vibration. A mass more than a hundred feet long wafted skyward, pausing above them and revolving in place. Then it descended at the same speed it had risen, raising no dust as it landed. Garland watched with reverence and awe. Even to the eyes of another mage, this was *unreal*.

"…Like flipping an egg to you, huh?"

"And now, observations."

Gilchrist stepped onto the air itself as if a staircase lay before her, looking down at the newly revealed side of the machine god's remains. Garland nodded and began inspecting the golem's lower half from atop the hilt of his broom.

"They're likely inspecting it by now."

At the same time, on the first layer, the ringleaders of the faculty murder were speaking.

"Not a problem. All wounds on that giant have been doctored to look like wyverns and the lindwurm."

"I know that! It was rough work covering up the evidence," a female student said, shaking her head. "The golem itself was damn heavy—no way to move the thing. Had to burrow tunnels under and put everything His Majesty hit back the way it was. Adamant is tough enough to work with, and we had to put up barriers, keep people away, and work through the night to get it done. Only reason we made it is 'cause you and Shannon remembered the exact locations of every scratch."

"Only Chloe Halford's Gladio is capable of slicing adamant," Gwyn said as he brewed a potion for his cousin. "Like the fourth spellblade, just seeing those marks would be enough to link us to her. We knew the cleanup would be rough going in… But our teachers aren't about to let us hide *everything*."

With that grim proclamation, the door to the room swung open. Both students looked that way and saw their lord standing there, looking very upset. Shannon glanced up from her writings and jumped to her feet.

"There you are, Noll... So the side effects have manifested?" Gwyn said. "Over here. Lie down."

He took his cauldron off the fire and beckoned Oliver to a gurney in the next room. Shannon came over and nestled herself close to her cousin, who promptly yielded to her examination.

"It just feels...off. Like the surface...has been *repaired*."

They'd been examining the golem for a good ten minutes before these words escaped Garland's lips.

"Your instincts were always good," Gilchrist said, nodding from the sky above. "There are distinct signs of magical modification. It was merely an impression on the top side, but the back has had minimal interference; they likely had to tunnel in, unable to flip the golem."

That made a lot of sense to Garland. Having found what she was looking for, Gilchrist dropped back to the ground.

"This proves the boy did not blow himself up. Enrico fought and was bested. That much is certain."

Garland nodded and hopped off his broom. If Gilchrist had nothing more to say, that meant there were no more clues to be found here. Whoever was responsible was clearly as skilled at subterfuge as they were in combat. Mulling that over, he asked the loaded question.

"...Who do you suspect?"

The witch merely shook her head. As he had anticipated.

"All I know now is that it was not *me*. There are signs of a cover-up, but we should not read too much into that. We can't even say for sure the minimal processing on the back is not an intentional ploy to mislead us. Make not haste; make your foe show their tail. Hence the investigation," Gilchrist said. "Still, whoever this killer is…they will not be sitting on their hands and waiting for us to make the next move."

Early the next morning…

The Kimberly campus had an area reserved for magical creatures. The section where Marco had been kept a year ago currently housed the griffins, and Katie had become a regular visitor. Magical biology classes often met here; depending on the time of day, there were a lot of students moving in and out.

But at this hour, with dawn barely broken, only a few ever ventured near. Chief among them was Vanessa Aldiss—the magical biology instructor so terrifying, the students had nicknamed her "the Tyrant." Her work duties naturally meant this area was her domain.

"Aw, shut yer traps. You ain't roosters. Or do you *want* me to roast you for breakfast?"

The cries and growls of sundry creatures stopped dead the moment they sensed Vanessa coming, her presence so palpable, they instinctively grew quiet. Her every motion was rife with violence, conscious or not. She strode from cage to cage, making her morning rounds.

But something felt amiss. She knew full well how loud manavians were in the morning and which cages should be the loudest at this hour. Yet, one particular cage was quiet as a tomb.

"…Hah?"

Vanessa turned toward it, peering through the bars. She found the griffins flat out on the ground, deep in slumber…seemingly just as she'd left them the night before.

"…Hmm…"

But that was not slumber. The moment she realized not a single griffin was breathing, Vanessa *knew*—what had happened here and for what purpose.

"Oh-ho, taking a run at *me*, are ya?"

Her right arm transformed, twisting the bars of the cage. When her palm opened again, the metal fell to the ground, crumpled into a ball like a wad of paper.

Several others had the misfortune to be in the animal pens that morning.

"Okay, okay, good, good! Keep it up. Now this way— Augh?!"

The griffin's wing had batted Katie aside, knocking her down. The young griffin she'd been trying to lead around glared at her a moment, then lost interest and turned away.

Miligan was watching Katie's struggle from a safe distance, arms folded.

"Hmm, it sure has your number."

"Erk... B-but still! It doesn't *attack* like it used to!"

Katie was soon back on her feet, ready to face the griffin again—but the Snake-Eyed Witch stepped in.

"Now, now, let's keep our heads about us, Katie. This works just like it did with Marco. We can't forge a healthy relationship when they're frightened of us, but likewise, we'll get nowhere when they're looking down their beaks at us. It seems like you've managed to convince the griffin you aren't an enemy. The next step is to persuade it you're more than an equal."

The griffin saw Miligan approaching and backed away, hackles raised. Clearly, it had sniffed out that she was not to be trifled with. With Katie, it lacked that defensiveness—which was an advantage— but it had a distinctive derisive streak that rather undermined that. Seeing her stuck between a rock and a hard place, Miligan had proposed they work together.

"And that requires a demonstration of power. In nature, a powerful foe inspires fear, but a powerful ally generates trust. Seeking friendship from a position of power will not be refused so lightly."

"...But I don't want to hurt it," Katie said, fists balled up tight.

Miligan smiled, nodding. "You won't bend on that point. I know. We have to demonstrate power without a direct attack. That *is* a challenge."

They fell silent, thinking it over. The three of them—griffin included—were at a stalemate. Then heavy footsteps came their way. The girls turned to look and saw a tall boy leading a troll in their direction.

"'Sup. Thought I'd drop by."

"Guy? Er, why is Marco with you? Out for a walk?"

"That too. But I had an idea. You're struggling with the griffin bonding, yeah?"

Marco moved toward Katie. The griffin could hardly remain indifferent to this troll-size threat and spread its wings—a gesture of intimidation.

"KYOOOOOOOOOOOOOOO!"

"Whoa…!" Katie cried. "W-wait, Marco. You'll scare it. Best to keep your dis—"

"Nope. This works. Let him get close."

"Wha—?!"

Unsure where Guy was going with this, Katie's head spun; Marco stomped up to her side. He glanced down at the griffin, who flinched—and fell silent, folding its wings once more. Miligan watched avidly, stroking her chin.

"…Hmm. Might not work on a mature griffin, but at this stage of development, Marco is a clear superior. It *knows* it wouldn't stand a chance in a fight."

"Unh… Now what, Guy?"

"Right there is good. It's your turn, Katie."

"Huh? Me?"

"Have Marco put you on his shoulder," Guy said, grinning.

Blinking, Katie looked up at the troll. "Uh, okay… Marco, do you mind?"

"No mind."

Marco nodded and held out his hand. Katie stepped aboard, and he gingerly lifted her to his shoulder. She was soon seated at his eye level. Seeing the griffin's gaze glued to this whole process, Miligan figured out the plan.

"Interesting approach," she said.

"Not something the griffin can just ignore, right?" Guy chuckled. "Here's something much stronger, obeying her directives."

Violence was hardly the only way to demonstrate strength. Having powerful creatures serve you was proof of superiority. Miligan had to admit the strategy had merit.

"Katie," she called. "Try bringing Marco along the next few times you interact with the griffin. Be careful not to give the impression of borrowed authority—make sure it sees him obeying *your* directives."

"O-okay!"

Katie also had it figured out now, and from Marco's shoulder, she began pointing, telling him where to go. The sight of Marco doing just that was likely making a big impression on the griffin. Its gaze never left them. One eye on that, Miligan slipped over to Guy, jabbing him in the ribs.

"Very clever, Guy."

"Thanks. When she's facing a creature, nothing else enters her head, huh? I figured it'd never occur to her to put Marco in the middle."

"Yes… I should have thought of it myself," Miligan said, rapping the side of her head.

Katie yelled down from Marco's shoulder, "The looks it's giving me are totally different! I think it's working!"

"Well, great. Still…"

Guy's gaze ran down her person. Scrapes on her hands and arms, dirt on her uniform, grass in her curly hair. Clear signs of the struggle so far. He put a hand to his brow, sighing.

"…Never mind. Keep it up!"

"? Don't be weird."

Katie shot Guy a baffled look, then gave Marco another directive. Guy observed her, stone-faced, and Miligan raised an eyebrow at him.

"...Holding your tongue?"

"You know, so don't ask."

"Heh-heh-heh. I suppose I do. You're certainly minding Katie's moves."

"It's more like she *doesn't*, so *someone's* gotta."

Miligan shielded her eyes with one hand, like he was too bright and she couldn't bear to look.

"Ahhh...she doesn't lack for options."

"What?"

"Never mind. Just thinking out loud."

But no sooner had the words left her mouth than every living thing present shuddered.

"____?!"

"......!"

They couldn't move. The tension was so great, they could barely breathe. And the moment they realized this stemmed from something coming up behind them, all eyes were drawn toward it: Vanessa Aldiss, both arms ominously swollen, taking big strides their way, eyes raking across human, troll, and griffin alike. Three different species all registering the same hopeless threat.

"...KYO...O..."

Her eyes bored into the griffin specifically, and its mind registered her as inescapable death. A threat so great, it did not dare to *run*, let alone fight. Its animal instincts spoke loud and clear—from this range, it was already caught in her jaws.

"...A-ah!"

Yet, in the midst of that uncharted pressure, Katie alone took action. She dropped down from Marco's shoulder and stepped out in front of the others. Like with Darius the year before, this was proof of her remarkable will. Here, however, she was but a lump of meat placed before a starving carnivore.

"…You gave…permission! What…do you want from us, Instructor Vanessa?"

The instructor's palpable hostility scorching her face, Katie attempted to communicate with words. Here was the sole hope of every living thing present that *wasn't* Vanessa. If words wouldn't work, no other options existed. Resistance itself was futile. Even unintelligent creatures knew that to be true.

"…This one's alive."

Thus, when actual words were offered in return, their looming deaths made a swift retreat.

"…?"

"Carry on. Miligan, keep an eye on things till classes start."

And with that, Vanessa turned on her heel and stalked away. Once she was out of sight, Katie's knees buckled. Guy and Miligan each caught an arm. She was damp with a cold sweat, like she'd been caught in a midwinter shower.

"……What…*was* that…?"

"She's…not usually *that* intense. Even my shoulders were quivering," Miligan said, speaking for them all.

Katie took Miligan's arm and pulled herself up—then sensed that she was being watched. The griffin's eyes were on *her*, a look of wonder in them, as if the creature was staring at something it could not comprehend.

"…Were you scared? Don't worry. I won't let her do anything to you. Ever."

She reached out to it, her tiny hand gently brushing its feathers. And this time, it didn't shake her off. Something had changed within the manavian without anyone—Katie included—realizing it. Or rather: Perhaps this was curiosity. Curiosity toward a far smaller creature who had faced certain death and driven it away.

A shadow passed over them, and Miligan looked up. Beasts were flying overhead: fully grown griffins, wyverns, and the like. Their eyes scanned the ground—this was undeniably ominous.

"Watchers in the skies," Miligan muttered, her voice grim. "Something's *clearly* amiss."

They found out what exactly was amiss the moment everyone gathered for breakfast.

"…That's…awful…"

Katie's fork fell to her plate with a sonorous clatter. Conscious of Katie's emotions, her conscience demanding she not mince words, Chela kept her tone flat.

"I'm afraid it's true. The griffins the second-year students were training have all been found dead. Only one survivor—the one you were looking after."

Katie's shoulders trembled. She started getting to her feet, but Chela stopped her.

"Deep breath, Katie. The faculty is already on the case. Those griffins were Kimberly property, and they aren't about to write off the loss. You saw the beasts on patrol above."

Her voice was soothing and well-intentioned. Katie knew she couldn't spend the whole day with her griffin, however worried she might be. But the storm within was not subsiding. All those lives lost without warning—she couldn't keep the anguish from her voice.

"…It doesn't make sense! This place is ugly sometimes but especially lately. Why kill all those griffins?!"

"Is this part of it?" Pete asked. "The teachers—"

Chela put a finger to his lips. She then spoke a warning, not just to Pete but to everyone seated with them.

"You must not. You must not speak a single careless word. I trust you know why."

Silence settled over the table. Beneath it, Oliver's hand felt a squeeze from another person's hand.

"No cause for alarm," Nanao said, her smile warm.

"...You two have been hand in hand since you got here," Chela noted with a smile of her own.

"I insisted."

"Hee-hee. I envy that. But I do think it's needed."

Her voice revealed her concern for Oliver's condition. And that only added to his hurt. He hadn't directly ordered the griffins' deaths, and yet—the moment he heard the news, he knew it had been his comrades' work. Meant to rile up Vanessa Aldiss.

"Until things settle down, avoid moving around alone," Chela advised. "Not just in the labyrinth but on campus as well. Try to stay with someone you trust. Katie, Pete, I'm talking to *you*."

"...I know."

"Less time in the library, then..."

They had their own thoughts on the matter, but neither blew off Chela's admonition. The six friends ate quickly and rose to leave— and as if the Fellowship wasn't already buzzing enough, further news arrived.

"The headmistress has summoned President Godfrey!"

"I have no knowledge of this matter."

A resolute male voice echoed through the headmistress's office. Seated on a solitary chair in the center of the room was Godfrey, a daunting gaze upon him, yet his tone never wavered.

"Once again, I am not involved with the disappearances of Instructor Enrico or Instructor Darius. Neither is any member of the Campus Watch."

Each word had force behind it, as if demonstrating he had nothing to hide. And without that stance wavering, he shot a question back.

"Why would I even be a suspect? As president, I'm certainly in a position to move numbers, but as reasons go, that's a leap. Would you care to explain the logic behind this summons?"

"A simple matter of your personal offensive capabilities, Purgatory."

Her words like frozen steel, the headmistress's gaze bored into Godfrey. One could argue that sitting before this witch unquailed, retaining your faculty for speech, was a prerequisite for becoming student body president.

"Neither Enrico nor Darius would be bested by a rabble of ordinary students. But you alone—there might be a chance. Your name coming up was not a leap but an inevitability. But that does not equate to the depth of the suspicion. Take it as an affirmation of your talent."

This was likely the highest praise she was capable of offering. Godfrey did not look remotely pleased.

"This is merely one stage of our institutional audit," the headmistress continued. "You aren't the only student we'll be questioning. If you suspect anyone yourself, name them now. I have a high opinion of your performance on the council. Thus, I consider your opinions worth hearing."

"My job is to protect the students. Not suspect them."

He didn't even hesitate. With the culprit in hand, he might involve the authorities, but as the stage of mere suspicion, doing so would be a betrayal of the students he led. In Godfrey's mind, that truth was self-evident. And the headmistress knew that about him.

"Fine. I'd like you to relay a proclamation in my name."

"What would that be?"

Godfrey's eyes narrowed. He wondered what words she might offer under these circumstances. But her answer surpassed his wildest imaginings.

"The faculty are upping the remunerations and prizes for all divisions of the broom races, broom fights, and broom wars. The victor or MVP on the winning team will receive a fifty million belc cash prize and a dragrium crystal. The same conditions apply to the combat league leading into the next election."

"——!"

Godfrey's eyes went wide when he realized what that meant. And Esmeralda's next words fell like an ax:

"That will be all. You may leave."

"Godfrey!"

"You made it!"

Tim and Lesedi were waiting for him outside, looking frantic. That summons from the witch of Kimberly was clearly an interrogation over the faculty murders. There was no guarantee the suspect would emerge alive—and that was not hyperbole. They'd been prepared to bust the door down if they had to.

"...I'll live. Sure didn't feel like it in the moment, though."

He wiped the sweat from his brow, easing his friends' nerves. They gave him a moment to recover, then Lesedi dug in.

"They think you killed those teachers?"

Godfrey pondered that briefly. "It's more like...they're going one by one through every possibility. I was called in first not because *I'm* their prime suspect but because *nobody* is."

"So a wide-range investigation, open to the idea that a student could be responsible... That means they're more in the dark than I thought. This isn't like her at all."

"Matters are clearly worse than we expected. Two lost Kimberly teachers in as many years is certainly unprecedented," said Godfrey. "...But she's taken action. The broomsport Big Three and the combat league before the election are all getting the prizes jacked way up. The victor and the team's MVP get fifty million belc and a dragrium crystal."

"Dragrium?!"

Tim's eyes gleamed like full moons. Dragrium was rare enough that any mage would want some, but that value skyrocketed if you were deep into alchemy. Tim's reaction proved that point and confirmed Godfrey's ideas about the headmistress's plan.

"That's bait, no doubt. Designed to drag more students into the school building."

"…Pretty costly bait. If that's all she's after, she could just hold a mandatory assembly for nothing."

"An assembly as part of an investigation is completely unnatural. A far cry from something that draws people out to begin with. This contest lets her demonstrate that Kimberly is business as usual. If any students stay hidden and don't take the bait—well, that just makes them likely suspects."

Godfrey took a deep breath, organizing his thoughts. He could see where things were going. Now it was their turn to act. He turned to the boy next to him.

"Tim, the dead griffins."

"I didn't do it!"

"I know. I'll negotiate with Vanessa and get permission for you to examine the bodies. I wanna know how they were killed. If possible, the time of death, too."

"We're running our own investigation?" Lesedi asked.

"No, merely pretending to. For now, I have no intention of pursuing the killer. This isn't like the cases we've dealt with. As long as there's a chance of faculty discord, us getting involved is far too dangerous." Godfrey then added, "But the griffin slaughter proves there's a chance this discord could spread to the student body going forward. We need to make the culprits think twice about doing that. So we make a show of looking into things."

Faculty problems were for the faculty to solve—Godfrey had no issue standing by. Their role was to ensure the students were left out of it. Lesedi nodded in agreement but offered one word of caution.

"Just don't forget the election's coming. And the headmistress just lit the fires under it," she said grimly. "The old student council members will be rubbing their hands together as we speak."

*   *   *

Just as the underclassmen gathered in the Fellowship, there was a hall for upperclassmen to do the same: the Forum, on the fourth floor.

"I, Percival Whalley, say this unto you: Godfrey's policies are fundamentally unsound."

A fourth-year student stood at the center of the vast hall, white wand in hand. Not an unusual sight as the election drew near, but the contents of his speech were rather provocative.

"In the labyrinth and this school building, the Campus Watch has protected many a student from harm. These successes have earned them a broad range of support, and at a glance, that seems like a positive. But think on it, please. What have their efforts given Kimberly?"

Whalley paused dramatically. Not to actually allow his listeners to think but to give the illusion that they had. The answer would be the one he provided.

"It is all too clear—the student body has grown *weak*. Kimberly is where all mages ought to stand on their own two feet—but now they find themselves clinging to the council's boots. The Watch have cast themselves as a source of unconditional aid. A veritable assault on the core tenets of this institute—freedom and results!"

His voice rose in fury. What had begun as rather fussy oratory was adding in one trick after another to whip his audience into a frenzy. His tone grew stronger still.

"If anything goes wrong—*talk to the Watch*. What say you to that? I say nay! Perhaps at some middling magic school, but this is Kimberly! We will not allow such namby-pamby nonsense to go unchecked! If a mage is in peril, they must carve their own way out! If you need assistance, you must pay the price, prove your interests are aligned, or resort to treachery and threats. By any means necessary! By following the principle of self-sufficiency! This is the way mages ought to be." He paused. "That is what I find so unconscionable about the current council. They seek no recompense! They dole out salvation to all students in kind, with no discrimination, no discernment! And no regard for the degradation it will cause!"

Whalley was arguing that his opponent's greatest merit was, in fact, the school's greatest shame. And that could not be dismissed out of hand. After all, this was *Kimberly*. An institute that had long been detached from the morals of the world outside.

"After three long years, we have a chance to correct this error. Vote for me in the coming election, and as student body president, I will restore Kimberly to its rightful form. Those of you lending your ears need not wonder who is worthy of your vote. You know there is no other choice. Not if you are a true mage!"

With that final exhortation, he wrapped up the speech. But instead of the enthusiastic applause he'd expected, a rather sarcastic clap reached his ears. He turned toward the sound and found a female student, hair covering one eye. A fifth-year girl running against him.

"A fine speech, Mr. Whalley. I *am* impressed. It was like traveling three years back in time. Amazing—to think the candidate back then said *exactly* the same things."

"...Vera Miligan."

"But I have my doubts about your claims. Have you even stopped to wonder why Godfrey felt the need to form his own council? How stifling this place was under your cronies and their rigid ideas of what a 'true mage' must be? Have a mere three years been enough for everyone to forget that?"

Before Whalley could answer, a man rose from the listening crowd.

"I don't deny that there was rot in our camp," he said, long golden hair glittering, half his beautiful features marred by burns. The kind of man who turned heads wherever he went. "But that is in the past. I have spent three years carving out that cancer—as I would have done had I been elected. Our institute does not suffer fools."

Leader of the previous council faction and Whalley's chief supporter—Leoncio Echevalria.

Miligan smiled. She had hoped to draw him out.

"It's a shame you never got the chance. Oh, have you still not healed those *burns*?"

In lieu of greeting, she chose to wind him up. The entire room froze. Whalley turned white as a sheet.

Leoncio dramatically put a hand to his brow.

"Ha-ha, ha-ha-ha. Ha-ha-ha-ha-ha. Miligan…"

"Yes?"

"Solis lux."

There was a sarcastic sneer to his voice, like he was trading jibe for jibe—but this was an incantation. He'd drawn his white wand so smoothly, Miligan was left unprepared. By the time she had her wand out, her vision was bathed in golden flames.

"Ignis!"

But fire from behind her pushed those flames back, the two forces equally matched. Two infernos clashing in the center of the hall. The flames neither spread nor sparked but instead *concentrated*. Vying for supremacy, they dwindled like a reactor core suspended in midair—and then they went out.

"…Put your wands away. The election is a distant prospect! Mind your tempers."

Alvin Godfrey stepped in, wand raised high. Leoncio greeted him like a long-lost lover.

"Ohhh! Godfrey. My beloved Purgatory!" he cried. "It has been *far* too long. But at last, I am prepared to invite you to my bed."

He put his wand away, holding out both hands and stepping toward Godfrey like a lovelorn soul. But the moment the gap between them shrank, a glass bottle sailed overhead.

"Go fuck a dog, asshole."

A potion hurled by *Tim Linton*. Everyone not part of the fight turned on their heels and fled for the hills. Anything *he* threw would be fatal

poison; their only chance of survival was to get out of range before the bottle cracked. And that would happen *before* it hit the ground.

Their expectations were thwarted, however—the rain of death never fell. An instant after Tim's throw, multiple glass spheres sailed from the opposing direction—all containing potions and all bursting in the same space as Tim's bottle. There was a violent neutralizing reaction that left only harmless smoke behind. Not a single drop of liquid made it to the floor.

"…I see you've made no progress whatsoever. Same old toxic gasser."

A fifth-year stepped forward, shaking his head. He'd customized his uniform to encase his slim figure in tights; his smile was gentle yet unwavering, designed to capture the hearts of all.

The tip of his wand aimed firmly at Tim, he continued. "I've said it before, but you have no understanding of alchemy. Poisons that cause suffering are but a failed by-product of the brewing process. Potions should heal, confuse, or drive others mad."

"Go back to polishing your tumblers, Barman. Your cocktails are too sweet for my taste."

Tim had his white wand out, too, and a new vial in his free hand. The old council's premier alchemist, Gino Beltrami—aka Barman— returned a look of pity.

As they faced off within striking distance, Leoncio snorted.

"…Your rabid mutt still isn't house-trained, I see. You should get on that, Godfrey."

Tim was so focused on Barman's face that he failed to notice the wand reaching over his shoulder.

"Fragor."

The spell hurtled right toward Tim's head, bursting before he could dodge.

"You're right—he needs it," Lesedi said, stepping in the instant the spell activated—and then deflecting the opponent's wand with her own. "But that's not permission for you to snap *your* whips."

The two white wands creaked, the wielders' faces inches apart—Lesedi's foe a degenerate-looking sixth-year elf, Khiirgi Albschuch.

"Such a terrifying scowl, Lesedi. Are you still holding a grudge about all those times I cucked you?"

"Are your lips only capable of emitting foul noises? Then their purpose is at an end. I'll sew them shut for you, Avarice."

Neither one of them was backing off. Three pairs, each evenly matched.

Seeing that, Godfrey spoke again. "Listen up, everyone! As president, I bring word from the very top: For the next league round, the headmistress is upping the rewards for all three disciplines. The winner or MVP from the winning team will receive a cash prize of fifty million belc—and a dragrium crystal. The same prizes are on offer for the combat league preceding the election. That is all."

Leoncio put his free hand to his chest, eyes raised in admiration.

"Our headmistress certainly knows how to gild a lily," he said.

"Pfft, she just extended the trough we'll fill with—"

Tim was quick to retort, but he stopped as soon as he started. And he wasn't the only one left speechless. Nearly every gaze in the room found itself locked on a single point.

"Exquisite. The perfect stage to make you *mine*."

"......!"

Even Godfrey gasped. His eyes were glued to Leoncio's nether regions; the cloth of his trousers had lifted to heights that made all doubt what they were seeing. Engorged with flowing blood, it pulsated like a beating heart—a member of truly prodigious proportions.

"Ahhh, the heat...! I can *feel* it, Godfrey! The mark you left on me is burning still!" Leoncio cried. "To extinguish it, I must tear everything from you! Rob you of everything you hold dear! Leave you dazed and confused, helpless to resist as I lead you to my bed. For days and nights without end, I will torment you, make you cry, make you groan, make you beg for mercy! I shall put a collar on your throat that shall remain there for all eternity!"

The man's lust was fanned by loathing and obsession, and he showed no compunction about voicing it all before his target. This was a declaration of intent. Arrogant, selfish—and in that, exactly how a mage's love *ought* to be.

"That day is not far off. Await it with breathless anticipation."

His eyes swimming with passion, Leoncio waved a hand at his clique and turned to leave, making no attempt to hide his cock's salute—no, he was proudly *showing it off.*

That same evening, the Sword Roses aimed to keep their word and inform Morgan of Ashbury's current well-being. Given the unsettling state of the campus, they decided it was best for *all* of them to go together.

"I am familiar with the three broomsports. But what is this combat league?" Nanao asked.

They were on the second layer, the bustling forest. Making their way through the trees, they were discussing the headmistress's proclamation—news that had arrived somewhat late, given all that had happened in the Forum.

"It's an official magic tournament Kimberly holds on a regular basis," Chela explained. "There are individual and team events, but I've heard in election years, the former is more common. The idea being to give the candidates a chance to demonstrate their personal prowess."

She paused briefly to cast a gust spell, mowing down the shrubbery ahead. Leading the party through the unobstructed path, she issued a warning.

"But that will be *next* year. The broom events are nearly upon us. Nanao, I'm sure you can post strong results in any of the three categories. If you intend to win, we should begin strategizing."

"You gotta go for it, Nanao! Fifty million belc! You know how much that is? You could live it up in Galatea for a month without breaking the bank!"

"Guy, don't be greedy! But it certainly is a lot of money... If only I was any good at riding."

"? Wait, *you* want money?"

"I'm not proud of it! But I could really use more, honestly. Given how expensive upkeep on magical creatures is...I can never have enough. Ms. Miligan also said it was high time I started thinking about my income..."

Katie let out a "life is hard" sigh. Research was often a huge money sink, and minor disciplines came part and parcel with budgetary concerns. She was going to be dealing with this struggle for a *long* time.

And hearing this made Nanao think.

"Then if I claim the prize, I shall offer it to you. I've no use for it myself."

"Nanaooo! You're *such* a good girl!"

Katie threw her arms around her friend, which stopped Nanao in her tracks—and since Oliver was holding her hand, it threw him off balance.

"...That *would* be nice," Katie then added. "But you can't. Keep the money. You may not need it now, but I'm sure it'll be useful someday."

She gave Nanao a firm pat on the back. One eye on them, Guy threw his arm over Oliver's shoulders.

"Nanao's going for it, so you'd better whip yourself back into shape quick."

"Don't rush him," Pete admonished, pulling Oliver's arm like he was trying to steal him away from Guy. "I read up on the subject, and a mage's slump is a delicate thing. You don't want him getting further messed up, do you?"

Since Nanao and Oliver had been holding hands the whole time, this left them at the center of a cluster—everyone but Chela clinging on to someone. The ringlet girl giggled.

"…Should I join in?" she asked.

"Please don't," Oliver pleaded. "Everyone, calm down! Give me some space; I can't exactly move—"

Mid-sentence, the foliage parted, and a burly upperclassman poked his face out.

"The gang's all here?" he asked.

Katie let out a little yelp. This must have been the Morgan they were looking for. Everyone quickly let go of Oliver—except Nanao, who was clearly adamant about this hand-holding thing. Chela stepped forward, speaking for the group.

"A pleasure to meet you, Morgan. I am Chela McFarlane, year two. I've heard you provided my friends with invaluable assistance, saving Guy from serious peril. I cannot thank you enough. Our friends here are Oliver Horn and Nanao Hibiya. Like myself, they've tagged along as a precaution—the school is a bit…agitated these days. That *does* make for rather a hubbub, but hopefully not an unpleasant one."

"Oh, so you're Instructor Theodore's favorite daughter? I can see the resemblance!" Morgan exclaimed. "You're all welcome! This was my request, so I appreciate your indulging it."

His eyes turned toward Oliver, who pushed aside the urge to hide his and Nanao's clasped hands and returned the greeting. It took only a few exchanges for them to feel like old friends; Oliver was relieved. This man was every bit as gregarious as he'd heard.

Before settling down to the main topic, they chatted about this and that, which naturally brought them to the current state of things on campus. Morgan looked genuinely surprised by the goings-on up above.

"Fifty million belc and a dragrium crystal? That's quite a bonanza."

"It seems likely the administrators have goals beyond making the league one to remember," said Chela. "But perhaps it's best we avoid further speculation on that topic."

"Definitely the right call. If the teachers are fighting, you under-classmen don't wanna be poking anything with a stick. Ignore the background noise and just enjoy the party."

Advice from experience. With that, there was a lull in the conversation, and Nanao seized the opportunity.

"If I may," she began. "I come bearing word on your lady Ashbury."

"Please. Hit me," Morgan said, nodding.

For the next few minutes, he lent his ear to her tale. When she was done, Morgan folded his arms, muttering, "...She still hasn't broken that record, huh?"

Nanao added her own impressions. "As a broomrider myself, I can speak to the importance of a catcher who is with you heart and soul. And to the timidity their absence can bring."

Morgan's eyes snapped to the boy at her side. "...He's your catcher?"

"That he is," Nanao said, proudly putting her arm around Oliver. This made him fidget, but Morgan just grinned.

"Every rider-catcher pair is different. Sometimes they stick together like you two; sometimes they spend the whole time arguing their heads off. But the one thing they all have in common is that no matter what happens—neither side can be replaced."

His eyes were focused elsewhere, staring into his own past.

"That was extra obvious with Ashbury. She'd had one catcher after another run off on her, until I was the only one left. Gah-ha-ha."

The memory made him laugh, but sensing their rapt attention, he let it die away.

"Honestly, I wish I *could* go back. But I can't catch anyone with my body like this. Showing myself to her now will just make things worse."

Morgan sounded resigned to his fate.

Katie looked hesitant to speak but couldn't stay silent.

"...Um, if we talk to the teachers, maybe—"

But mid-sentence, Morgan turned away, coughing hard. A burst of fire left his lips, curling upward and blackening the branches of a nearby tree.

"...*Ahem*. Sorry, what was that?"

".........Um...never mind."

Katie said nothing more. What she'd just seen was more potent than any hope she might offer. The man ravaged by tír fire was only too aware how little time he had—and that was *why* he spoke to them as people who still had lives ahead.

"You've already done more than I bargained for, but let me ask one more thing. Don't tell her I'm still alive. There's nothing she can do for me. I'm just an ex-catcher burning himself out."

That didn't sit well with anyone. But he wasn't about to let them dwell on it. The instant the mood got gloomy, Morgan's voice boomed.

"So light the fire in her! If she's up against a wall, then the best way to punch through it is to make her *extra* competitive. That's how she ticks. The next league'll be the perfect stage. All she needs is a *rival*."

He turned to Nanao. One of the few riders capable of entering Ashbury's zone.

"Take to the skies and face her down, Nanao Hibiya. That's all I can ask."

She nodded once. The heartache behind that request cut her to the quick.

As everything around him was in tumult, Oliver's condition showed no sign of improving. His cousins' examination hadn't helped much.

"Enough. Wand down, Mr. Horn."

It was bad enough that the teacher had to step in in spellology class. Oliver froze to the spot as Gilchrist approached.

"Your mind is adrift," she said. "Attending class in that state is a liability for those around you."

"...!"

He couldn't argue. The results before him said it all. The assignment was a transformation, one requiring fine control—but the glass he'd intended to roll out thin as paper was mottled and white. His inability to maintain the transparency showed how badly he'd failed to control his mana.

"Waving your wand around blindly will not help. Recovery cannot be *hastened*. Sit yourself down for self-examination. Do you hear me?"

And here he was getting "helpful advice" from one of his targets. Yet, there was so little light reaching Oliver that he couldn't stop himself from groping for an exit. He failed to find any hints on how to even begin the path to recovery; his days were filled with anxiety, panic, and failure. Class time was no different.

"Whoa, what's wrong, Mr. Horn? You're not usually someone who looks ready to fall off their broom. Did you break a few bones when I wasn't looking? Need a little healing, maybe? My spells hurt like the dickens."

Repeating takeoff and landing failures in broom class had Dustin genuinely concerned. The broom Oliver had been riding for years seemed perplexed, and he was struggling to even fly straight.

"Well…don't let it get to you, Mr. Horn. This was rather a tricky assignment. Even upperclassmen blow a brew if they've been away from a cauldron awhile. We all have bad days."

His brew in alchemy class was a complete write-off, and Ted's smile was very sympathetic. He had no confidence in the simplest ingredient prep, and the more cautious he got, the further away success became.

"………"

His group was all following different curriculums, so Nanao was not in the alchemy class with him. This itself was not unusual, but in Oliver's current state, it felt like the one guiding light had gone out.

"…It happens to everyone! Don't let it get you down."

"It wasn't even a big failure. Not like you blew up your cauldron."

Katie and Pete *were* with him and picked up on his mood. They tried to help, but all he could manage was a faint smile.

"Oliver Horn, Pete Reston."

All three had been in a hurry to meet up with their friends, and an icy voice struck them in the back at the worst moment.

"I have questions for you. Proceed directly to my office."

They turned like rusted machines. Her silver hair agleam, standing there in the gloomy hallway was the witch of Kimberly—Esmeralda.

Where Godfrey had sat earlier, the two boys found two chairs. They took their seats feeling like prisoners on death row. Standing at the window, her back to them, the headmistress began.

"You've heard about Enrico Forghieri's disappearance."

"Only rumors."

"…Same."

It took a lot of strength for Oliver to get those words out, and Pete followed his lead. The witch watched out of the corner of her eye.

"Shortly before his disappearance, you two visited his workshop, yes?"

That explains it, Oliver thought. He chose his words carefully.

"…Yes. Pete was invited, and I insisted on joining him."

"Elaborate on what you saw and heard. Leave nothing out."

As ordered, Oliver gave a rundown of the events. Pete's invitation had seemed risky, so he and Nanao joined them, overcoming the trial Enrico had set to reach the workshop itself. There, they'd been shown Dea Ex Machina. All this was likely in the notes Enrico had left behind, so he had no intention of hiding anything.

When he finished his story, the witch turned toward them, snapping, "You loathed his work."

Oliver's heart leaped out of his chest. He had been sure he'd left out all traces of his bias, but he'd certainly revealed his distaste for Enrico's work to the man's face. He couldn't allow for that to make him a suspect.

"......I didn't...exactly—"

Trying to recover his poise, he started stammering a reply—but a chant echoed through the room, and the back of Oliver's chair fell off. He and Pete sat bolt upright, watching as the headmistress sheathed her wand once more.

"This is *my* inquiry. Do not speak another meaningless word."

Only now did the shudder catch up with him. She'd severed the back of his chair *through* his body, allowing him no response to the chant itself—and without harming a thread of his robes. Should she have so chosen, she could have sliced his body to pieces.

"...H-Headmistress!" Pete's voice was a squeak, every part of him shaking. And yet: "Y-you suspect Oliver and I had something to do with his disappearance, don't you? Th-this is part of the investigation, right?"

Her silence signaled agreement. A wave of fear hit them, like their heads could leave their bodies any second. Pete pushed through that, stringing words together so that he might live.

"Can I ask the estimated time of the incident? Between the last sighting of Instructor Enrico and the discovery of his disappearance? I have a good memory of my own activities that day. What Oliver and I were doing, who we were with—who can vouch for us."

An orthodox approach to proving innocence. Pete kept talking, not letting Oliver help.

"I heard it took place on the fifth layer. I've never been that deep inside the labyrinth, but I'm aware that even for a skilled mage, it's not somewhere reached in a short amount of time. We should be able to provide alibis."

"No need."

His life depended on these words, and she dismissed them out of hand. Pete stopped breathing.

"You are in your second year. I do not for a moment believe you slew him yourselves. I am speaking to you regardless for the simple reason that Enrico's Deus Ex Machina *was* taken down. Do you realize what that means?"

Her blade turned back toward them. Seeing tears at the corners of Pete's eyes, Oliver took over.

"If I may clarify something… We were shown a golem called *Dea* Ex Machina. An unfinished prototype with no lower body. Is this the same construct you called *Deus* Ex Machina?"

"What you saw was a second model, still under construction. What was destroyed on the fifth layer was a previously completed model."

"…Okay, then… Your culprits are very good and likely more than one."

"Worse. That invention was hardly something multiple skilled mages could hope to eliminate," she corrected, moving directly beside him. "I believe the killers had *thorough* knowledge of the machine god *before* the fight began."

Oliver felt his stomach twisting into a knot. He knew full well she was right.

"…And you suspect we leaked that information?"

"That is one possibility. Though a separate model, the invention was shown to you. And Enrico did not show off his work without a basic explanation of the functionality. That knowledge would make all the difference in taking it out."

He had nothing else to say. A long silence hung between them before Pete managed to recover enough to speak.

"I understand why we're here. But I'm certain we are not the only students Instructor Enrico showed his work to. And it was supposed to be only me there; Oliver invited himself along afterward. Since the instructor allowed that, I think it's safe to assume he showed it to many other students."

"You talk a lot, Pete Reston."

This was praise, not a snide remark. Formulating a clear rebuttal required analytical skills, as well as the gumption to continue speaking even while shaking in fear. Pete was accomplishing something any Kimberly student could be proud of.

"Your reasoning is sound. You are not the only students invited to view the machine god. That is why I said 'one possibility.' The two of you visited the workshop right before the incident in question, and one could argue that students who visited the workshop long before the incident are far more likely suspects."

Feeling like the pressure was lifting, Pete blinked—but the witch's next words slammed it all back down.

"Yet, at the same time, you said it yourself—Oliver Horn was *not* supposed to be there. He *invited himself*."

Pete looked like he'd been struck by lightning. He had *never* been the target of this investigation.

The witch's gaze turned to Oliver—back to him. To the prey she'd always had her sights on.

"Enrico gave you a considerable challenge. Not one any ordinary second-years could ever overcome. Yet, overcome it you did, earning you the privilege of viewing his work."

"......!"

"What made you *that* curious, Oliver Horn?"

Only now did he fully understand why suspicions had come his way.

Certainly, other students had viewed the machine god. But the vast majority had demonstrated magical engineering excellence and were invited there *by Enrico*. Someone *asking* to visit his workshop was clearly exceptional. And Oliver was not generally a particularly enthusiastic magical engineering student. Given what had happened after, finding his motives suspect was entirely natural.

The panic was making him sick to his stomach. He racked his brain for an explanation. What could he say that would alleviate

these suspicions? If he simply said the truth—that he'd been worried about letting Pete go alone—how would that sound? Would that lousy answer satisfy this witch? He suddenly grew very conscious of the severed back to his chair. Cold sweat left his clothes clinging to him. If the next utterance he made was deemed meaningless, her subsequent spell would slice—

"We merely accompanied our friend out of concern for his well-being."

It felt like a warm breeze against his back.

That settled everything. She'd spoken for him, saying what he'd hesitated to admit. No second thoughts, no trace of contention. Only *with pride.*

"We had no other motivations, Headmistress. Does that answer meet your needs?"

Standing straight as a pin, the girl stepped beside her friends. Pete called her name as if handed a lit torch when lost in darkness. "Nanao…!"

The Azian girl stood between them, directly staring down the witch of Kimberly. As she did, Oliver's eyes caught a glimpse of something on the headmistress's face that had not been there before—a brief twitch of her brow.

"…Leave this room, Nanao Hibiya. You were not summoned here."

"That is most strange. Three of us attended Instructor Enrico's workshop—Pete, Oliver, and myself. If the two of them are under suspicion, then I must be as well. Am I not?"

Her tone was as soft as her stance was firm. No trace of hostility or reticence. She sounded as if she was speaking to a friend. *That,* in all likelihood, was what perplexed the headmistress. Not a single student had dared this kind of approach since she began her reign over Kimberly.

There was a long silence. However—it was clearly not like the silences that came before. This was not a silence designed to intimidate; it was simply the result of someone struggling to make up their mind.

"…Today's inquiry is over. You may all leave."

And when the witch spoke again—there was a trace of a sigh in her tone.

They'd escaped the witch's grilling with their lives. No exaggeration—that was how *both* boys felt.

"*…Hahh, hahh…!*"

"……"

They staggered down the hall outside her office and dragged themselves into a first-floor lounge. Pete collapsed on a chair in the corner, chest heaving like he'd been running for his life. Oliver had his head down, not moving a muscle. Nanao was standing behind them, stroking their backs.

"You are safe now. You have my word."

"I'm making tea!" Katie said, stuffing leaves in a pot.

If they headed to the Fellowship, they'd find Chela and Guy and all the food and tea they could want, but neither boy was capable of walking that far yet. A few minutes in the headmistress's office had left them thoroughly exhausted. As far as an audience with the witch of Kimberly went, this outcome was likely extremely fortuitous.

"…You really saved us," Pete rasped. "I dunno how much more I could've taken…"

Nanao smiled and shook her head. "I should have been there from the start. Credit must go to Katie, who thought to fetch me."

"Nanao, you said you had tea with the headmistress before, right? I remembered that, and then I didn't stop to think more. I'm so glad it worked out!"

Katie wasn't taking her eyes off the pot, waiting for the tea leaves to unfurl. And while they waited, Pete finally managed to catch his breath.

"...I can't believe...you can just talk to the headmistress like *normal*," he said, staring down at his cup as Katie filled it. "Every answer I gave, I felt like I was teetering on the edge of a cliff."

Relieved to see Pete was on his way to recovery, Katie glanced at the other boy.

"You want some, Oliver? It'll help you relax. I put in a *lot* of jam."

She handed him a teacup laden with apricot jam. Tea culture had spread to every part of the Union, and this particular style was popular up north. Oliver took it listlessly, but the heat rising from it proved irresistible, and he took a gulp.

"...Nn..."

Sweet, hot liquid slid down his throat and warmed his stomach—and as it did, big tears spilled from his eyes.

"...Er...?"

Katie had been prepping a third cup for Nanao; Pete had been taking a sip from his own. Both saw Oliver's tears and froze to the spot. He sat hunched over his warm cup, his tears making the surface ripple as he sobbed soundlessly.

"...Sorry...I couldn't...do anything..."

Apologies spilled out of him. He wanted to curl up and disappear.

"Nanao stepped in to save us. Katie went to fetch her. Pete kept the headmistress arguing until she got there," he said. "But I didn't do anything. I just let her cow me into submission, sat there shaking like a leaf, not even able to explain myself... Just letting all of you protect me..."

Once he got started, there was no stopping his remorse. Katie flailed about for a moment, then pulled a handkerchief out of her robe and started dabbing Oliver's tears.

"...Oh..."

And from that close, she made a new discovery. When this boy cried, he looked *far* younger.

"...I never had any *real* strength. Not compared to the horrors in this school... But that's *exactly* why losing what little I have is so damn scary. Walking down the halls, speaking out loud...just *breathing* is absolutely terrifying now...!"

Everything he'd been trying to hide was tearing out of him. And that put the same metaphor in both Katie's and Pete's minds. It was like a heart made of crumbling clay, exposed and floating before them.

Both moved without thought. They couldn't *not* put their arms around him. They knew how often he'd protected them, and they couldn't let him fall apart.

His body was cold to the touch—painfully so. Neither Katie nor Pete said a word; they just held their trembling friend tight. And Nanao put her arms around all three, like she was a blanket laid upon them. They stayed like that until the steam stopped rising from their cups.

"...Oliver, let us repair to our base tonight," Nanao said at long last.

She flashed a toothy smile, as if that alone could banish all his fears.

"I have a notion by which we might proceed."

That same evening, they'd collected Guy and Chela, relocated to their secret lair, and were once again discussing the gravity of Oliver's condition. Whatever this was, it obviously wasn't just going to go away on its own. That much needed to be clear to everyone.

"......"

When the initial discussion concluded, Chela rose to her feet. She moved around the table to Oliver's side—and took his hands, almost falling toward them.

"...This is *my* oversight. We should have picked this apart and dealt with it long ago. How could I have been so blind? I should have known how dire this was the moment you dueled Rossi in sword arts class." She went on. "I am so, so sorry... I can't apologize enough, Oliver. Here I claim to be your friend, yet...!"

This had hit harder than anything since she enrolled here. She had looked the other way when her friend was suffering, and the resulting guilt brought her to her knees, shaking her more than any spell. She cared for him yet had come up short—and that realization made her heart bleed.

"...No... No, Chela..."

He managed a whispered denial, but even that had no strength behind it. With no way of resolving this matter on his own, he couldn't find a way to comfort her. Their friendship was going in circles, connecting nowhere, and Guy couldn't bear to watch.

"Okay, okay, deep breaths, everyone. Why do you folks have to be so dang hard on yourselves...?" he grumbled. "It doesn't matter who missed what or when we knew. What matters is putting our skulls together and figuring this out. Let's do *that*."

Here were two friends prone to overcomplicating things, so Guy offered a simple solution. Rather than dwell fruitlessly on bygones, they could put their minds to making things *better*. That sounded immensely appealing. Katie and Pete were both nodding.

"Guy speaks the truth," Nanao said. "And I do not believe this matter is as insurmountable as you fear."

Sensing her confidence, Chela wiped her tears, asking, "Really? Nanao, you know how to cure Oliver?"

"'Cure' may not be apt. But as my people say, 'a single sight is worth a hundred words.'"

Invoking a saying from her homeland, she began spelling out the specifics of her solution. They would use the base's main hall, normally split into four quarters—Marco's room, Katie's animal pens, Guy's garden, and the indoor exercise room—as one large space. Together, they moved everything—animate or not—aside. This took nearly half an hour.

"Mm, that should do it. Marco, if you could just stay in the corner..."

"My planters are all good. I'd just harvested everything anyway.

And we put softening spells on the whole floor like you said—but why, exactly? We gonna be doing some tumbling?"

They'd done as Nanao asked and found themselves in the middle of a vast springy floor, like a gym covered in mats. She nodded her approval and turned to the others.

"You have my thanks. Now we are ready to play at being demons."

At what? said every face there. Sensing they weren't familiar with her term, Nanao gave them a rundown of the rules, and they were soon nodding.

"...Ohhh, you mean like tag," said Guy.

"Where I'm from, we call it catch and catch," Pete mentioned.

"Fascinating," Chela added. "To think Yamatsu children play the same game!"

"But...why now?"

Nanao just grinned at Oliver's question and said, "'A single sight is worth a hundred words,'" again. Don't think, do—apparently. Still somewhat perplexed, Oliver nodded. Best to take her word for it.

"With standard rules, whoever the demon catches becomes the next demon. I'd like to suggest a deviation there. The demon makes catches but remains a demon—thus, as the game progresses, the number of demons increases."

"Oh, I've played by those rules!" Katie exclaimed. "The last player has to run like crazy from *everyone*!"

"So how do we score it? Wouldn't that mean the game ends with *all* demons?" Guy asked.

"Precisely. Thus, there are neither winners nor losers. As humans, you flee as best you can; as demons, you endeavor to catch the survivors. That is how children play."

Play for the sake of play—not for bragging rights. With the objectives clear, Nanao turned her back and covered her eyes with her hands.

"I shall serve as the first demon. I will now count to ten—so I suggest you all start running."

She began counting, and the others spread out across the open space. None of them went too close to the walls—they needed room to maneuver as the demon closed in.

"...Seven, eight, nine, ten... Ready or not—here I come!"

Nanao spun around and made a beeline for Katie, who quickly turned and ran...albeit a bit *too* predictably. Nanao turned ahead of her, closed the gap, and her palm slapped Katie's shoulder.

"A-already?!"

"You are now a demon yourself, Katie!"

"Argh, then let's get everyone! Grrr!"

"Whoop...!"

Katie had flung herself at Oliver like a wild beast, forcing him to leap backward. She had leaned too far forward and went head over heels, but that was why they'd softened the floor; it caught her easily, and she bounded right back to her feet.

"...That didn't even hurt! I love it! We can go all out!"

"Pete, your back's unguarded!"

On the other side of the room, Nanao's palm was closing in on the bespectacled boy. She'd caught him against the wall, and just as he seemed to have nowhere to run—his feet carried him diagonally *up the wall*. Nanao let out an impressed cry. A few steps later, Pete lost his balance and was back on the floor near Oliver, who stared wide-eyed.

"...Crap, I can't get past three seconds. Need more practice."

"Wall Walking? Pete, when did you—?"

"If I've seen it, I've practiced it. Obviously."

Pete was already running off. Those shoulders seemed far sturdier than when they'd first met—but before Oliver could marvel at that further, his gaze landed on Nanao, and he was forced to run again. He incorporated a sideways feint to get her off his tail.

Meanwhile, Katie was throwing herself into this whole demon thing. She'd switched targets to Chela, lost her, and then got Guy cornered by the wall. Neither one was moving a muscle, just staring each other down—and it was hard to go into a Wall Walk without any momentum. Guy had two choices—left or right. And Katie was hell-bent on nabbing him, whichever path he chose.

But Guy was not so easily tied down. He drew his white wand, chanted a spell, and used the ensuing smoke cloud to slip past her. As he ran off, he yelled over his shoulder, "Nobody said no spells!"

"Augh! Cheap trick, Guy! Is that even allowed?!"

"As long as the spell won't hurt anyone, I rather think so," said Chela. "Do you agree, Nanao?"

"But of course!"

The rules expanded by request. Oliver grimaced at that, but come to think of it—this was how children's games *worked*. Their feet nimble, their minds free. He sensed a touch of that youthful whimsy coming back to him—and felt a pair of arms close around his chest.

"Eh-heh-heh-heh-heh. I caught you, Oliver."

"…Yeah, you got me," he said more ruefully than he'd expected. Even as he switched to the demon role, he swore not to get caught next time. He hadn't yet realized just how into this he already was.

Meanwhile, Katie had been after Chela again, but when she spotted Nanao's arms around Oliver, an idea struck her.

"…Oh! Catching someone means you can *touch* them."

"An excellent interpretation, Katie," Chela called back, their minds as one even as they fled. With three demons, Guy didn't last long. Chela held out to the bitter end but was soon surrounded and fell. Without pausing for breath, they went into round two.

"This time I'll serve as the demon. Commencing the countdown!"

Chela covered her eyes and began the next round. The other five took positions, putting what they'd learned to use, mindful of the expanded rules.

"…Nine, ten. Here I come!"

She turned around and set her eyes on Pete, who had—fascinatingly—placed himself in the corner. Clearly, he had some sort of plan in mind, and that piqued her curiosity—so she headed straight to him.

"Clypeus!"

Wand in hand, he made a protrusion high above, then used the triangle jump principle to kick off both walls and get high enough to grab it. He pulled himself up onto the protrusion, looking down at Chela below.

"How's that? If you try and climb after me, I can knock you back with a gust spell."

"...Interesting. You've made yourself a safe spot to camp, rather than running willy-nilly."

"It goes against the spirit of the game, I know. So I intend to try it out this round and go with something else next time."

From his perch, he had his wand ready—and Chela smiled back at him.

"Don't worry, Pete. You won't have to."

And with that, she put her foot on one wall—not running like Pete had. Just strolling up it, like she was on level ground—perpendicular to the wall. The bespectacled boy's eye twitched.

"...You...can do that?"

"Watch and learn. I'm not yet a match for my father—but *this* is a *real* Wall Walk."

The gap between her and Pete's perch was closing fast. He recovered enough to make good on his gust spell threat, but she effortlessly neutralized with the oppositional element. Even mid–dramatic Wall Walk, Chela still had the capacity to sling spells.

"...Argh...!"

This perch was no longer safe. Pete used a blackout spell to blind her and tried to jump down the side she wasn't on. But he couldn't disguise his intentions, and Chela jumped into his path, wrapping her arms around him as he fell.

"Wah?! C-crap...!"

"You're the first! Now, if you'll excuse me."

"...Um, h-hey—"

In her arms, Pete looked flustered—but Chela paid that no mind, giving him a good squeeze. He found himself surrounded by warmth and soft flesh and went very stiff. The embrace lasted a full ten seconds before Chela finally released him. Where Pete was positively fossilized, her smile gleamed.

"What a wonderful game, Nanao. We can hug our beloved friends as much as we like!"

"?! No, wait! Hugs are in no way necessary!"

"Strictly speaking, no. But neither is there any rule against it. Much like your spell use, Guy."

She'd clearly expected his argument and came prepared. Guy quickly gave up. He'd expanded the rules first and couldn't really gripe if someone else did the same.

"Awww…you got me! Now *I'm* a demon!"

Katie went down two minutes later. She'd definitely been running for real but didn't sound remotely disappointed to be switching sides. Her eyes caught Oliver's across the room, and she grinned.

"…You don't mind if I get a bit rough, do you?"

"…Sh-sheesh, Katie, you sound like you've got ulterior motives!"

Oliver backed away; Katie's grin made her look like a carnivore sighting dinner. She lunged toward him—but Guy stepped between them, wand raised.

"Not so fast! All rules in moderation."

"You can hug whoever *you* like, Guy! I won't mind!"

"Like hell I can!"

"Then you're next, Guy!"

Chela jumped into that fray, and the game sped up. The girls became fearsome hug warriors, and the boys were forced to flee their dreaded embraces.

Three hours straight of working their bodies to their utmost. No one had infinite stamina—not even mages.

"...*Hahh... Hahh...*"

Pete was on his back, breath ragged. He'd been the first to go down, but Katie and Guy soon followed. The three of them were all slumped together by the wall.

"...Well? You satisfied...? Having your way...with me...?"

"...You kept on...butting in, Guy... I wanted...to catch Oliver more...!"

"...You're not even...trying to...hide it..."

"...Friends can hug! It's not...weird..."

Guy and Katie were arguing through their panting, but three of their friends were still going strong. They didn't look remotely tired—in fact, now that the players were more equally matched, they were going even harder.

Pete managed to pry himself up off the floor enough to see, muttering, "...How are they still moving? It's been three hours... No breaks..."

"Yeah... Even off his game...we're still no match..."

"...But..."

Katie frowned, looking over again. Her gut was nagging at her. Everything here appeared to be as usual—but something had changed.

"...was Oliver...always that fast...?"

The boy himself had not yet noticed.

"...*Huff... Huff...!*"

Oliver was in a white-hot high. His mind purely on the game afoot, chasing, being chased, a world of pure simplicity. No room for anxieties or fears.

The severity of his condition, the possibility it could not be cured—all such thoughts were banished. He spared not a thought for what lay ahead, simply running moment to moment. Dodging right, leaping left, feinting down but leaping overhead instead—and Nanao's hand got his ankle anyway.

"Caught you!"

"…One more!"

"Then I'll be the demon!"

The next game began the moment he landed. With only three players left, the rules had tightened up; no more spells, but "caught" now required a "hold" on any part of the body. Even if a demon got your back against a wall, if you could push past them without them grabbing on, you were free.

"Hahhhh!"

Chela's hand snaked out, and Oliver deflected it with the back of his own hand. They traded feints a moment, neither gaining an advantage. All three had trained in hand to hand, so this was almost a martial-arts exchange. Only the demon could "grab," but anyone could "deflect." Get good enough, and you could go toe to toe with the demon. But even these rules were not enough to satisfy their thirsts.

"I'm all warmed up now! What say the demon has to get their foes pinned?"

"The yielding arts! Now that tickles my fancy!"

"I'm in! From here on out, getting your opponent's back on the floor is a 'catch!'"

A few exchanges later, Chela caught his arm and turned from him, both hands going for Nanao, who wasn't backing down. They grabbed for sleeves and hems, skill against skill from any stance.

"Sword arts is too often about immobilizing opponents…but going hand to hand like this is a thrill all its own!"

"Don't bite your tongue, Chela!"

As they fought for balance, Nanao suddenly shifted. Her right hand caught the sleeve by Chela's elbow, her left the collar—and with those held firm, she spun her body, her back against Chela's front. Chela flew upward, twirling overhead before landing on the floor again. This was one of the Hibiya-style yielding arts Nanao had learned back home.

"…Oliver!"

"...Come at me!"

Those words proved enough, their minds aligned. According to the rules, neither was a demon right now, but that had ceased to matter. They were children at play. And they played as their hearts led them.

"...Shaaa!"

"Raaah!"

They clashed, blood boiling. A moment's lapse would leave him sailing through the air, and Oliver threw himself into turning those tables. His spatial magic was now uselessly inaccurate, so he cast that out, reading his opponent's tells, biding his time to counter her moves.

She turned that back on him, too—baited him into a throw or a leg sweep. He hit the floor twice, then three times, bounding back up for more each time without stopping. Neither even considered it.

Nanao almost had his arm, so he jumped. He felt an elbow coming at him and bent himself just in time.

"Ha-ha...! Submission moves aren't in the cards, Nanao!"

"My apologies! I was enjoying myself, and my body acted out of turn!"

She let go of the arm she had twisted behind him, laughing. A furious exchange of blows followed by collar and sleeve clutches, then more skills on parade. Her left hand forced his elbow down, and then Nanao half spun into the boy's bosom. The move she'd used to throw Chela! Even as that registered, Oliver was already in motion. Not fighting the flow of power but flinging himself in the direction of the throw, keeping himself in control in midair, and getting his feet down on the floor.

"...Hng!"

"Hahhh!"

Nanao let go and righted herself, but Oliver turned that against her, attacking. In quick succession, he used three leg moves designed to push her down, and when her center of gravity was leaning forward in response, he switched his off hand from her wrist to her collar.

He spun himself into *her* bosom, grabbed her right arm from below, and jerked his hips up. First, incapacitate the dominant hand—the hand holding the athame. A Lanoff-style sword art move devoted to that principle—the throwing technique Break Wheel.

The sound of her hitting the floor followed. Nanao lay there on her back, and the momentum of the throw left Oliver tumbling down beside her. They lay together, gasping for breath.

"Magnificent," she said.

The others had been watching in awe, and they all scrambled to their feet, rushing over.

"Oliver, did you…?"

"Uh, you just *threw* Nanao!"

"My man! You've got your groove back, right?"

Guy said it all. To their eyes, Oliver's movements had been getting sharper and shaper. He'd been too lost in the moment, but in hindsight, he felt it, too. His body *worked*. He knew *how* it worked. The nagging uncanniness that had plagued him, the feeling that he was trapped in someone else's body—all that had faded away like it had never been there to begin with.

"…A simple matter," Nanao said. "When your body changes, you need only move it. Dwell not on moving like you once did. Cease restraining yourself with notions of how you *should* move. Leave your mind behind as your heart guides you, like a child racing across the fields."

She was still flat on her back, but she turned her head toward Oliver.

"Your body and mind were not aligned. That is all this ever was," she told him. "Oliver—you did not *lose* strength. You *gained* it. You gained so much power that you could not operate as before—and entirely unawares, at that."

Oliver let those words wash over him like sunlight. Nanao's explanation proved insufficient for the others, who all turned toward the ringlet girl.

"…Translate that, Chela?"

"…A significant improvement to the mana circulation in a short period of time. As a result, how he need handle his mana is dramatically transformed in a way that leaves his consciousness one step behind. I believe that's the gist."

"That happens?"

"……I can't rule it out. We *are* all growing mages," Chela replied. "Just—as far as I can remember, Oliver's mana output had been *steady*. Incremental increases in line with his body's growth, but no signs of such dramatic leaps. Given that it left his own mind behind, this is clearly a remarkable case. Perhaps there was some trigger outside of our knowledge."

There were still mysteries involved, but that was all the analysis Chela could offer now.

As everyone turned to him, Oliver muttered, "…So I'm *not* weaker?"

"Not a whit. You are, in fact, stronger than before."

"Then I haven't lost…lost everything I'd built."

"The heavens and earth could switch places, and that alone would not betray you."

Nanao spoke with authority. The foundations he'd laid remained within him.

"…Ah—"

His throat shook. His vision blurred. Emotions welled up within—ones he could not hold back.

"Ahhhhh…!"

Even as the emotions assailed him, he knew why he had so feared losing his strength.

Without that strength, he couldn't fulfill his desire. He couldn't avenge his mother or do anything for the comrades who'd fallen. Each of those reasons was accurate and yet not *all* there was to it.

The strength he had was inherently corrupt. Borrowed from a greater soul, the result far too warped to even dub a facsimile thereof. As the mad old man had so viciously decreed, his blade scarcely resembled what Chloe Halford's own soul had been capable of. Once stained with hatred, no matter how he polished it, it was never more than the sword of a killer.

And yet—despite all that, it *was* a link back. His love for his mother, his admiration for her, his efforts to be like her... There was strength gained from that, too. He could look back and see his warped footprints in the sand, but if he followed them backward, it would take him to that shining past with *her*. However deep in darkness he now was, he knew there was still a path leading back to the light.

No matter how mistaken the nature of it was, the *bond* remained.

"Unh—ah—"

Thinking of days he could never have back was making his soul scream. *Oh, Mother, how I loved you.*

Even though he had changed so much—though his nature was altered forever, the madness of that love alone remained.

"...Do not cry, Oliver. This is not the time."

Nanao sat up, looking ready to cry as well. As the boy grieved, she pulled herself on top of him, brushing his cheeks with her fingertips.

"I cannot bear it. Cannot bear to stand uselessly by, watching these tears flow."

Her face moved in, and her lips touched his. Like a lid upon his tears.

"Uh, Nanao...?! ...?!" Katie yelped, but Chela reached out a hand and held her back. The look on her face made it clear she would brook no interference. This was not a moment anyone else could be a part of.

Guy and Pete felt the same. They held their breaths, watching.

"...Bwah...!"

After a long, long time, Nanao pulled away. She'd kept their lips together as long as she had breath, and now her shoulders were heaving, her cheeks flushed.

Oliver looked up at her, and she rasped, "...My apologies... I knew no other way to calm you."

She had allowed herself to act and felt a tinge of shame. Her fists clenched, her eyes wavering between sense and sentiment, she stood ready to accept any rebuke.

And gazing up at that, all Oliver did was smile. "I don't remember us making any rules against kissing when caught."

Those words freed her from remorse, and he followed them by putting his arms around her. Brushing her head, soothing her, he patted her back with his other hand and poured all the affection he had into it.

At length, their embrace ended, and they stood up. Oliver turned to his other friends.

Guy spoke first, still rattled by these events. "Should we, uh…give you two some space?"

"Don't make it weird, Guy."

Oliver slumped right over to his friend and threw his arms around him. Guy was too shocked to produce sounds with any meaning.

"Uhhh…?!"

"We're still playing demons. Hugs are all part of the rules. Right?" Oliver whispered. Then he tickled Guy's ribs. Guy screeched and Oliver let go, turning to Pete.

The moment their eyes met, Pete looked away.

"Hmph," he said. "Almost a pity. We fixed you so fast, I didn't get a chance to protect you myself."

"No, you absolutely did, Pete."

Oliver put his arms around Pete, who was attempting at a brave face. The bespectacled boy kept his expression resolutely cross, but from within his robes, where no one else could see—his hand clenched Oliver's shirt tight.

His third hug finished, Oliver turned to Katie. Realizing what was about to happen, she started backing away.

"…Er, um…Oliver…"

"Let me have this one, Katie. Even if I get a bit intense."

He spoke over her and smiled from ear to ear, cutting off her escape. His embrace showed no mercy. It was *very* intense. His hands moved like he was petting a puppy.

Once Katie was down for the count, he handed her off to Nanao and turned to Chela—last but not least.

"…Chela, when I'm feeling most like saying sorry, you always come and apologize."

"…Yes, it's a habit we should both try to break."

Wincing a bit, the pair reached for each other. Chela was doing her level best to act natural, but deep down, she'd been fighting to keep control. Overjoyed at seeing her friend in good spirits again, she was one step away from acting *just* like Nanao.

"…Uh-oh," Oliver said, letting her go. "I feel like a single round of hugs isn't nearly enough."

It was as if her own desires had rubbed off on him. Chela puffed out her chest proudly. "Then by all means, keep going. Get all the hugs you need. Or…why not? What say we agree that within the Sword Roses, we have a free hug policy?"

"What in the heck…? It's not like tea or coffee!" Guy groaned.

Chela was smiling brightly but clearly *not* joking. Everyone picked up on that…and was forced to give the proposal serious thought.

An eye on one another's reactions, they began responding.

"…Fine, but only with fair warning," Katie said. "I'd want a moment to prepare."

"…I'll push you off if I'm not in the mood. The rest of the time, go ahead."

"I have always hugged whosoever I pleased."

With Pete and Nanao on board, Oliver was now nodding, too. Guy remained the extreme minority. He blinked a bit, saw the expectant looks, and threw in the towel.

"…Argh, fine! Knock yourselves out. Just don't yell at me if I'm sweaty."

Possibly a touch of sour grapes, but everyone started grinning, and then all of them threw themselves on him at once. He tried to run, but Katie pulled him in, sniffing.

"……Hee-hee-hee, you *do* smell a bit sweaty."

"Don't worry," said Chela. "I'm sure we all do."

"Whoa, not all at once! The bath! Someone run the bath, please!"

Guy's yowls filled the lair, and everyone laughed.

When one petal faltered, the others held fast until it could recover. The flower their swords made still bloomed strong.

CHAPTER 4

Ashbury, Fleetest of Heart

Two years and several months prior, on the labyrinth's fourth layer—the Library of the Depths.

"……"

Within a tower bursting with books, in a corner reserved for reading, a man sat buried amid a mountain of forbidden tomes. Oblivious to the shadow approaching from behind.

"……Hey, nitwit."

"……………Mm? Oh, Ashbury."

Morgan turned and found Ashbury hovering on her broom, looking particularly disgruntled. He waved a hand dismissively but soon realized the deeper implications and put his chin in hand.

"You're here alone? That's pretty risky."

"Because you didn't come back! The next league starts in two weeks! How long are you gonna hole up down here?"

He knew all that, which was pushing her to the brink. Seeing the library guardians turn toward her voice, Morgan clapped a hand over her mouth.

"Sorry, sorry, has it been that long? My research is at a critical stage. I got lost in the details, planning the experiment."

That was news to her. Ashbury brushed off his hand, scowling.

"The experiment? You won't tell me much, but it's tír related, right?"

Her eyes shot through him, and he folded his arms.

"Given what lies ahead, you have a right to know. Okay, come take a look."

It depended on the research topic, and there were shared lairs, but for the most part, mages never invited anyone to their bases. And not for lack of personal connections, either. Thus, this was the first time Ashbury had set foot in Morgan's workshop.

"I've been studying Luftmarz. Based on the cycles, that tír should get close four months from now. I'm planning on carrying out my big experiment then."

Morgan had his hand on a massive glass sphere at the back of the room.

"I intend to open a micro-Gate in this and summon fire through it. I'll be observing and analyzing the flames to fully understand their nature, with the goal of placing them under my control. That's the gist of the experiment."

"...The moment I heard 'tír' I had an inkling, but...that's risky as hell. One false move with the Gate, and it'll be a disaster. Even if that part works out, do you actually have a legitimate shot at getting tír fire under your control?"

"If I didn't, it wouldn't be much of an experiment. And this is all approved by the faculty. I've pored over all prior research on the subject and made sure I've eliminated any possible errors made in the past. I'm confident enough I can pull this off," Morgan insisted. "But nothing in this world is certain. That's why I'm giving you a heads-up. Whatever the results, once the time is here, I'll be holed up in my workshop for at least three months. You'll need someone to take over for me, right?"

At that suggestion, Ashbury tore her eyes off the sphere, glaring at the man.

"...Four months from now, you'll go down to the labyrinth, and three months later, you'll come back up."

"At a minimum, yes. Assume it could be one or two months more."

"Then let's go with the full five. I won't wait another day. Keep me waiting beyond that, and there's no place for you on the Swallows. No matter who argues otherwise, I won't let you back," Ashbury told him. "So promise me you'll emerge unscathed. And that you'll be my catcher again next year."

The harshness of her terms concealed a simple wish—his survival. That was her way of offering encouragement. Morgan grinned back at her.

"Always planned on it. Don't you crash and die while I'm away."

"Who do you think you're talking to?"

She swung a fist, but he caught it in his palm. Like he'd known she'd react that way. It was so smooth, they both had to laugh.

She waited. But the promised day came and went without his return.

The league match was about to begin. The broomsports arena stands were packed with students. Among them walked a small boy, his face hidden behind long bangs as he pushed his way through the crowds.

"...Er, coming through... Do you mind...?"

Each time he met a wall of people, a whispery voice emerged. That would be one thing if this worked, but most students were too busy talking to even notice him. He was forced to tug on people's sleeves and get their attention.

"...Coming through... In a hurry here... If you could just let me pass..."

This mostly earned him baffled looks. Some stubbornly refused to stand aside, but when that happened, he had a last resort—his armband. Flaunting that got him shocked looks and always opened a path, but today, he hadn't needed it. He threaded his way through the last of the crowd, reaching a table. The broomstick flying instructor was already seated at it and waved him over.

He took a seat, offering a simple greeting. Before him lay the arena's field and the sky above it. Opening-act riders were executing fancy maneuvers for the crowd's entertainment, and he could *feel* how primed this audience was for the main event. The boy slipped a hand into his robe's pocket, taking out a small box. Inside was something goopy, and he scooped out a bit, rubbed it on both hands, then brushed his hair back from his hairline.

That switched him *on*. He took a deep breath, used his wand to cast a voice-amplification spell, and yelled, "On your feet, savages! It's tiiiiime—for the broom fight senior league!"

His voice cracked across the stands like a whip to a sleeping behemoth. This was Roger Forster, Kimberly's star broomsports announcer.

"Some of these first-years might not know the rules, so here's a brief rundown! While broom wars are all about teamwork, broom fights are one-on-one battles showcasing each rider's skills! No tricky dogfights or side fights here! Only head-to-head bullfights! Every clash could be the end! And I can't get enough of it!"

All traces of his timidity were gone, blown aside the moment he sat down and put his hair back. Nobody loved broomsports more, nobody got more into each twist and turn, and that's why he was so good at whipping the crowd into a frenzy. That was Roger's style.

"Our analyst today is Instructor Dustin! Things are real crazy on campus right now, and I'm sure he must have a lot on his plate, but he took time out to make this first day a good one! A big ol' thanks to you, sir! Can we get you a cider?"

Roger handed him a cup (it was already on the table), and Dustin glared at him. The dark circles beneath his eyes made it clear he hadn't been sleeping much.

"...Make it an ale. One of those extra-hoppy brews from up north. And put it in a mug the size of a sink."

"No booze in the booth, Instructor! But even as we speak, the first match is getting started!"

Roger dropped the banter, focusing on the match ahead. In the skies above, two riders had started their descents. As they passed each other, their clubs clashed. The impact shook both, but they soon recovered, speeding up, skimming along the surface, and rising again. The crowd whooped as they headed higher, ready for the next clash.

"Whew, they aren't holding back today! Beverly Lonergan versus Monique McKay! They've fought before, and their record stands at six to four! Dustin, what's your call?"

"Two veterans showing how it's done. Whoever wins, we're in for a long haul. And while they're at it, we should teach the younger kids a thing or two. What's the founding principle of broom combat?"

"Your commentator can handle a pop quiz, no problem! The answer—speed makes altitude, and altitude makes speed!"

"Exactly. It's easy to fixate on the clashing clubs, but that principle is still active here. The better you are at flying, the better you are at fighting."

Dustin was in full teacher mode now, and Roger knew just what response he was looking for.

"But, Instructor, flying in this sport looks so simple! One goes to the top right, the other to the top left, both turn together, rocket back down, and BAM! Then they switch sides and go again! If that's all you're doing, does flying skill really make a difference?"

"Yes, and a clear one. First of all, when they clash together, whoever is flying faster will have a major advantage. They hit harder! Which means both riders here have to think about how much speed they can pile on before the hit."

Dustin's eyes never left the match. Up, down, clash, up, down, clash. Tracing a figure eight through the sky, both players were constantly vying for the speed advantage. They were gaining speed and keeping it.

"The most important moments come when you're moving from a descent into an ascent or vice versa. A lot rides on their cornering and their sense of timing. A bad turn means a loss of speed, and a loss of speed means they lose the advantage at the clash. And that disadvantage isn't just that *one* clash, either. These blunders tend to add up over time."

And that cumulative effect was obvious even to an untrained eye. Each rider was tracing an arc through the air—and when those arcs were matched, the bout had yet to tip in either's favor. But as the speed disparity opened up, the symmetry broke down. The rider with the speed advantage traced the bigger arc, while the slower player's arc shrank. The longer the bullfight went on, the more inevitable that became. The clash was set at the midpoint between them, and as they both headed toward it, the player at a speed disadvantage was inevitably at a lower altitude than their opponent.

"The nature of this event means the path of the turn and the timing of it change each time. The impact of the clashing clubs always causes some discrepancy in the flight trajectory. They have to decide in the moment how to minimize the loss of speed while correcting that and how to gain as much speed as possible before the next hit. They go back and forth a bit before a decisive gap opens up, but that is the basic flow of a broom fight."

"Makes sense! It may look simple, but it's packed with technicalities!"

"Exactly. And that gap's starting to open up here."

The battle had raged on as they spoke. Six clashes in, the player on the right was starting to trace the larger arc. An advantage a mere correction of speed or altitude could not overcome. This was the second phase of a broom fight and where the crowd started wringing their hands, sweating the results.

"As the gap in speed widens, it gets harder to turn the tables. Once things end up like this, the disadvantaged rider has only one option— try to end things before that gap becomes insurmountable. As you're about to see."

The disadvantaged competitor on the left had shifted her grip on her club. A small motion to be spotted from the ground, but not one Dustin or other veteran observers would let pass unnoticed. At full speed, the pair plummeted toward each other, their shadows passing. The crack of club on club was extra loud—and the rider heading right did not ascend again. Her body was off the broom, dropping straight down, snagged by the catcher below. The crowd roared.

"Down she goes," said Dustin. "She went for an Encounter, but her opponent hit her with the same move. That could still pay off if you've got the sword arts skills, but…eh, this time, things went as well as expected."

"Lonergan wins the clash! She kept her accumulated lead and rode off with the victory! The catchers have escorted the plummeter off the field, and the second-round players are entering! We don't waste time between matches in the broom fights! Don't worry, people—your favorite riders are coming right uuuuup!"

"Using the first match to guide new viewers—Instructor Dustin's zeal for audience engagement and expansion is as asset to us all."

Chela nodded, impressed. They were seated on the north side of the stands, directly opposite the commentary booth.

Watching the new contestants enter, Pete folded his arms.

"They really made that match easier to follow. But broom fight or broom war, they still haven't answered my biggest question—why do mage sports not involve spells?"

A natural question for anyone from a nonmagical background. Oliver and Chela both turned toward him.

"Why are there no spells in broomriding? Well, basically, that's asking why the broomsports rules settled on a variation *without*," said Oliver.

"Strictly speaking, there *are* variant rules that allow spells. There was even a time when that was the primary discipline. Yet, as time passed, the spell-less variant took to the fore."

"The path to that was anything but simple. But we can name two of the biggest factors: First, broomsports are, above all, games played *while flying*. Flying faster, better, smoother—that's what the riders strive for and what the audience craves. And that core factor works against the inclusion of spells."

"Why? Does casting disrupt the flying?"

"It makes you *slow*," Chela replied. "For the simple reason that you're feeding mana into your broom as you fly, so if you're casting, the broom itself receives less power. The deceleration is unavoidable. In a sport emphasizing speed, that's clearly less than ideal."

"...Oh. So allowing spells takes the shine off the flying."

"That's the first reason, yes. Additionally, we might add that hitting people with spells midflight is easier said than done. The exact challenges vary by type, but dogfight, side fight, or bullfight, the deceleration from casting leaves you at a disadvantage. So not only are you unlikely to hit anything, the attempt undermines your position."

"Meanwhile, blunt strikes with clubs take advantage of the speed. The faster you're going, the harder they hit. Naturally, the strike itself does cause a slowdown, but that just makes the battle all about finding ways to increase your opponent's speed loss while minimizing your own. And *that* means the match is about flying speed *and* skill."

Chela had brought it back to that core concept. Eyes on the match above, Guy nodded, mulling this over.

"If the brooms are the star of the show, the spells are just a distraction."

"Yep. And that's not just broomsports. Aerial combat with brooms—*real* fights—follows the same principles. If you've ever seen the Gnostic Hunter riders in action, the way they fight is a logical extension of broom wars and broom fights. A clear representative of that ethos is the existence of an athame built specifically for aerial combat—the balmung."

Oliver's descriptions of the Gnostic wars carried grisly implications, yet they brought a smile to Chela's lips.

"The balmung riders!" she said. "I heard the stories as a little girl. Many of us grow up on them."

"One of them's sitting right there in the commentary booth," Oliver said, shooting their broom instructor a meaningful glance.

Dustin Hedges was leaning back in his seat, scowling at the skies above, looking like any other die-hard broomsports fan. Yet, he had been one of the world's foremost heroes on the aerial front lines. It was hard to imagine now, and the attempt made everyone laugh.

"...Our turn's coming up, Nanao," Oliver said, getting to his feet. "We'd better head in."

Nanao was one of many entrants waiting for her slot; she and Oliver were already in uniform.

"Mm, let us proceed," she said, standing up. "Friends, we shall meet again anon."

"Knock 'em dead!"

"We'll be cheering for you!"

With those cries buffeting their sails, they ran off. Just as they were out of sight, someone stepped forward from the other exit, and Katie called out to her.

"Ms. Miligan!"

"Oh, there you are. I'm running a little late. I *meant* to be here for the first match."

The Snake-Eyed Witch was carrying a very large satchel. One eye on the start of the fourth match, she took a seat next to Katie.

"Pardon me. I assume Nanao and Oliver already headed out?"

"You just missed them!"

"That's a shame. I would have liked to wish them luck."

She shifted her satchel to her knees. Something inside it was *moving*. Guy shot her a quizzical look. "...? What's in the bag?"

"Were you aware that the league victors are allowed to make a speech before the crowd, Guy?"

That wasn't really an answer, but it was clearly relevant somehow. Guy's frown deepened.

"And during election seasons, the victors generally mention who they're voting for. If Nanao wins, I figure she would happily do that for me."

Miligan unzipped one section of the satchel, and Guy caught a glimpse of a cage within. Behind the bars: the face of an adorable bird.

"So naturally, I'll be offering a salute in return."

The arena's western clubhouse. From here, it was a straight shot down the corridor to the field; the room was currently packed with riders waiting their turn.

There was *some* tension, but their opponents were all in the club-house across the field, so nobody was starting anything here. They were focused on communing with their brooms, polishing their clubs, or kicking back with magazines.

"…Ready, Nanao?" Oliver asked, looking her over.

She was seated on the bench next to him, but in answer, she turned her head away.

"Far from it," she said.

"…Something bugging you?"

"My catcher has not motivated me sufficiently."

Oliver's eyes went wide. There was a long pause; then he reached out with both hands, snagged her cheeks in his fingers, and pulled.

"……Let's not get *needy*," he said.

"Nya-heh-heh."

She was giggling like a mischievous child. Oliver let go of her cheeks and drew her into an embrace instead. Feeling each other's hearts beat, they remained like that for a full ten seconds—and feeling the time had come, he let go. Nanao shot to her feet.

"Strength—a hundredfold! I must go fetch Amatsukaze!"

She raced off to the broom corner, and he grinned after her.

"…That's your true strength," said a voice in his ear. He turned to find a sixth-year girl standing there. She was on the Wild Geese with them—Melissa Cantelli, the team's vice captain.

Embarrassed by the scrutiny their actions had drawn, Oliver looked away, but she just smiled and shook her head.

"You have nothing to be ashamed of. Love between players and catchers is ideal. If your bond is unstable, so is her performance. And I've seen more than enough unstable pairings to know how that ends."

Realizing he couldn't just ignore Melissa, Oliver bent an ear her way.

"Ashbury's a good example. In her prime, she was something else. No one could stop her, no matter which discipline she was in. But when she lost her catcher, she was a wreck. I can't say I ever *liked* her, but it was still rough to watch."

"......"

"So go on and dote on Nanao all you like. Don't take that affection for granted, either. You can never have too much. A mage's desires know no limits."

What had started as advice from a teammate was swiftly deteriorating into a busybody aunt's fussing. Oliver's nod was rather wobbly. This failed to discourage her—if anything, she hitched herself a notch closer down the bench, whispering in his ear.

"...Are you taking time for sex? No skipping foreplay because you're tired, now. It's critical! You've gotta get her engines going or—"

"Stop!"

"What's all this?" Nanao said, returning with her broom just as the escalation proved too much for Oliver to handle. He jumped to his feet and grabbed her hand.

"Nothing!" he said. "Let's go, Nanao!"

He pulled her toward the field. As Melissa watched them go, a fist landed on the back of her head. Another sixth-year teammate—the Wild Geese captain, Hans Leisegang.

"Don't stick your beak that far in right before a match, numbskull. What if you get them all distracted?"

"S-sorry... I know, but when I see them together..."

"I mean, I get it. But I also like that about 'em. The way they're teetering on the brink, stopping themselves from taking that last plunge."

He glanced up at their retreating backs and grinned.

"Flowers like that don't bloom at Kimberly often. They don't even *bud*. I ain't gonna scold the nosy grandma in you, but some fur is best left unruffled."

"...I'll *try*. But it's just... Go for it already! Argh, I have so many tips to give!"

"That's just your pent-up frustration. I heard you had another lover bail on you?"

"Aughhhhh! Are you trying to start a war?!"

He'd hit a sore spot, and Melissa made a grab for him. Hans ducked away, calmly glancing after Oliver and Nanao once more.

They had stopped at the line on the floor, waiting their turn. A few minutes later, the official ahead of them flashed the sign, and they hopped on their brooms, flying the rest of the way. As they entered the field, the lights blinded them, the roar of the crowds buffeting their ears. This was a moment that turned many a rider into a lifelong addict.

"Mm? Oliver, over there."

Nanao had turned her eyes toward their friends and spotted something odd. Letters being written in the air—by a number of birds flying above the stands, the glowing tips of their tailfeathers leaving trails in their wakes. A few moments later, the message was complete: *Good luck, Nanao Hibiya.*

"…Ah, that must be Miligan," Oliver said, figuring out the trick. He soon found the Snake-Eyed Witch seated near their friends. Nanao waved back, and Oliver grinned. "Perhaps not the purest of motives, but she *is* hoping you'll emerge victorious. Let's take it at face value."

"Mm!"

It certainly seemed to have lit a fire under Nanao. Spotting her opponent and his catcher, Oliver ran through the final reminders.

"You're up against a fourth-year endurance fighter. Tends to deflect club strikes, draw out the match, wait for you to slip up. He won't bite on a direct clash in the early- *or* mid-going."

"Then I shall just have to *make* him."

Nanao shot him a confident smirk; he grinned back. She headed upward, and he headed down to his post on the ground.

"I'll be watching you win down below, Nanao. Go get 'em!"

"On my word!"

*   *   *

Two figures rising, one right, one left. And the crowd cheered for a single player—the announcer louder than anyone.

"She's here, she's here, she's here! The girl you've all been waiting for! Arrived at Kimberly in spring of last year, never held a broom before her first flying class—and barely a year later, she's already tearing up the senior leagues! Making waves like no one around, it's Nanao Hibiya! Give it uuuuuuuuuuuuuuuup!"

"You get way too hyped when Ms. Hibiya's around. You haven't even mentioned her opponent!"

"Don't worry—I haven't forgotten. She's up against a fourth-year named Arnaud Jonquet! He's also a young hopeful of the senior leagues, having moved up in his third year. Can he hold on to that title against his opponent's dizzying rise?"

The horn sounded, and the match began. Both players shot downward, clubs clashing together at the heart of the field. The blows were so hard, they rattled their very bones. Nanao went right and Jonquet left, but Nanao already had the *clear* speed advantage.

"Baaaam! Jonquet failed to deflect *that* hit and struggled to keep control! Hibiya's already in the lead!"

"Ha-ha! Hibiya's figured out to lay the pressure on. Guess wielding a two-handed weapon *every* day helps there! Even the best player would have trouble deflecting a strike like that."

Dustin was grinning like a maniac. He may have ribbed Roger for it, but he was clearly more than a bit keyed up himself. No matter how long you'd watched or how much you knew, when Nanao was in the air, it was impossible to react otherwise. Every eye in the house upon her, she steered her broom back into the skies above.

"They've completed their post-clash turns and are headed into a second plunge! With the speed advantage, Hibiya's also coming in from higher up! This blow will be even stronger than the first!"

"It's only clash two, but Mr. Jonquet needs to show his mettle here. If he loses this clash, the fight will be entirely at Hibiya's speed. Hang in there! You can't afford to hold back!"

Dustin got a bit *too* carried away and forcefully slapped the table. His eyes were locked on Nanao's and Jonquet's approaches. They passed, their arms swung—with shocking results. The instant their clubs clashed, Jonquet's broom went into a wild spin. Unable to maintain flight, he was flung helplessly toward the ground. Nanao swooped off to the left, making a beautiful turn and easily ascending once more. The outcome was all too clear, and the audience was left gasping.

"Ohhhhhhh?! Jonquet falls! That hit had him spinning like a top! Hibiya wins on the second clash! A much faster bout than anyone expected!"

"He went for the Koutz Tour, and it backfired. I applaud the decision to play his ace this early, but he clearly hadn't practiced it enough to use on Hibiya. Perhaps it might have worked on the first clash, but we'll never know."

Dustin was scowling now, pinpointing the cause of this result. The refs confirmed Nanao's victory, and she waved at the stands before descending toward the exit tunnels.

"Day one of the league, and Hibiya started things off with a stunning victory! Awash in the roars of the crowds, she's back on land. But oh, it was not nearly enough. We can't wait to see you fly again! You there, fly up and put the sun to bed! Go round the world once and make it tomorrow for us all!"

Landing in the exit passage, Oliver soon caught up. They high-fived, then headed down the hall on foot.

"…That was a fast one. But not as easily won as it looked, right?"

"Mm, the second clash was a turnup. Had that move been a tad more polished, I may well have been the one downed."

"That's a high-level Koutz move. Don't think he's ever shown that in a match before, so probably still practicing it. Don't forget how it felt— the next time you face him, it'll be that much stronger."

But as they discussed the match, they saw someone up ahead. Diana Ashbury was leaning against the left side of the corridor, a vicious grin on her face.

"Your first match, and a two-clasher. Think you're a big shot now, Ms. Hibiya?"

"You were watching, Ms. Ashbury? Fortune favored me. My opponent made his move early."

"Riiiight, 'cause you forced his hand."

Ashbury cackled merrily. Then she turned away, calling over her shoulder.

"The rest of these gnats don't matter, but be there for my fights. They'll be worth the look."

She put that promise into practice not ten minutes later. When the crowd saw the Blue Swallows' ace take to the air—they fell silent. Their mouths became dry.

"Just the sight of her puts tension in the air. She needs no introduction! Empress Diana Ashburyyyyyyyyyyyyyyyy!"

"She's been focusing on broom races, improving her time, but still entered the broom fight league. Very like her."

"She's up against a sixth-year, Lauro Scarlatti. Their record stands at eight to two, Ashbury advantage. Instructor Dustin, what do you reckon?"

"His recent matches show Mr. Scarlatti's in good form. While Ashbury's been out of the fight *and* war rotation. We'll have to see how that affects her."

"Does the Empress's club still live? Oh, and the round is a go!"

The players on the field had started their descents. Everyone assumed the first clash would be feeling each other out—and that assumption was *trampled*. Her opponent put the momentum of the dive into a swing of his club, but Ashbury left hers resting on her shoulders. Not swinging at all, she shot in close—and his swing caught empty air. As Ashbury flitted beneath his arm, the tip of her club caught him, dragging his body *the wrong way.*

Pulled off his broom, his body sailed through the air, falling to the ground below. A catcher's spell caught him, and he lay there stunned, unable to process what had happened to him. His eyes were locked on the sky, where Ashbury was already headed to the exit tunnel, heedless of the crowd.

No cheers, no applause, not even any gasps. The stands were *silent.*

"...............................What?"

"You're breaking character, Announcer! Not that I blame ya. The senior league is full of heavy hitters, but it's rare to see anyone downed on clash one."

Dustin's voice was hoarse. The very nature of the format made a one-shot victory exceedingly unlikely. Even with significant skill discrepancies, the most you'd see was two or three clashes. But there *were* shock attacks specifically designed for that, and Ashbury had just demonstrated one. They were a rare sight in high-level bouts, more the stuff of acrobatic maneuvers.

Generally, Dustin was not a fan of such cheap tricks. They went against the intended purpose of competing on the merits of your flying skills. But this time—he was forced to see it in a new light. He was all too aware Ashbury had used the move in answer to Nanao's two-clasher earlier on.

One was the only number less than two. That was the sole motivation behind her decision. By pulling off a move harder than threading a needle, she'd proven her continued claim on the throne. She hadn't used the surprise to steal an unjust win—she'd *chosen* a one-clasher from a broad range of paths to victory. How could anyone complain? "Impressed" was the only option.

"It's often said the three broomsport disciplines are one and the same. Races, fights, or wars—practice in any of them leads to strength in the others. Naturally, everyone places greater emphasis on one or another, but Ashbury has always made that tenet clear. She improved her race times by knocking people out of the sky. And now she's done the opposite."

That was what had brought the Empress back to the leagues. Here, Dustin slapped his own cheeks, and the noise startled Roger, who turned to look—and found the circles under the instructor's eyes had vanished.

"Ashbury and Hibiya woke me right up. This league's gonna be a wild one."

That evening, they gathered in the Sword Roses' secret base to celebrate Nanao's victory.

"You made it through the first day! You're the coolest, Nanao!" Katie cried. Everyone clinked glasses—Marco's was more a wooden barrel— and cider droplets flew.

Chela wet her lips, remembering the match. "A two-clasher—it certainly got things off to a lively start. Are swift victories the plan?"

"More like Nanao has no interest in giving anything less than her full strength on each hit," said Oliver. "We've decided to let her run with that. Results are all that matter, not the speed of them."

"Ha-ha, that's so Nanao! I like it! And this victory gives us an excuse to party all night!"

"Don't be ridiculous, Guy. Once we've eaten, we'll be *studying*. You've been slacking off on alchemy practice."

"Aw man, Pete with the wet blanket! How do you know what I'm slacking on?"

"Katie and I will get you up to speed. Isn't that great, Guy? You get to brew potions *all night*."

The mood remained celebratory. They talked about the matches today, who she'd face next—the chatter never ceased. And the party lasted well into the night.

By three AM, everyone but Oliver was in bed. He slipped out from his covers, careful not to wake anyone, and exited the base.

He soon left the first layer behind and stepped into the bustling forest. Breathing in the smell of wet leaves, he cautiously picked his way through the woods, hurrying to the base of the giant irminsul tree within.

"*Huff... Huff...*"

A root bulged from the ground and connected to the towering trunk above. Before he climbed onto it, Oliver took several deep breaths, consciously accelerating the circulation of both blood and mana. Making sure he was at peak performance from the first step.

"...Good to go!"

Warmed up, he checked the hands on his pocket watch and broke into a run. Soles pushing off the bark with force that surprised even him, his body bounding higher and higher, the uneven terrain proving no obstacle.

(*My Lord! I'm afraid—at that speed, I can't keep up!*)

Teresa's warning came over their mana frequency, and the yelp in her voice was a genuine surprise. His covert operative had far more experience racing through the labyrinth than he did. Barring extreme circumstances, he'd never once managed to outpace her.

(*...Fine, remain on standby! I'll call if anything comes up!*)

(*Yes, sir... I'm...sorr—*)

Her voice cut out before she finished. Without a path created by a powerful contract, it was hard to maintain mental communication over long distances via mana frequency alone. He'd be out of touch with Teresa until she caught up—but conscious of that, Oliver maintained his speed.

"Phew...!"

When he finally stopped, he was at the peak of the irminsul—the highest contiguous point on the second layer. From here, you could see almost the entirety of the forest spread out before you. Wiping the sweat from his brow with the back of his hand, Oliver checked his watch again.

"Base to peak in thirty-two minutes. That's nearly ten minutes off my previous record."

That previous run had been recorded before the Enrico fight. He'd been well aware how much faster he was going as he climbed—he never got stuck. Tricky sections he'd been forced to take on hands and knees he could now run right through. And at that speed, the magic beasts avoided *him*. Perhaps it was also the right hour—he'd made it this far with little to no interference.

"...This is *definitely* no ordinary improvement," he muttered.

Like Chela had said, even a growing mage would never see *this* much physical enhancement over such a short period of time. You saw cases like Nanao's, but her baseline improvement speed was always "extremely rapid." Compared to her leaps and bounds, Oliver's growth had been unsettling, like a bug scuttling slowly across the ground— and then suddenly sprouting wings.

It felt *wrong* in a way that made one thing clear—this was a life-span *compression*.

A simple fast-forward could hardly explain it. Growth meant for the future had occurred preemptively—concentrated and poured into him *now*. His flesh and ether were running on that survival mechanism. His own soul had deemed him unlikely to pull through otherwise.

The trigger had clearly been the two-minute-plus merger with Chloe Halford's soul and the ensuing intense battle with Enrico Forghieri. His headlong rush toward the brink of death had forced his soul to reject itself. It grew convinced that the operations of flesh and ether it had planned—that is, a life lived typically—would not be enough for him to last another second.

The result was a fundamental alteration in his soul. To maximize the experience siphoned from Chloe Halford's soul, a swath of Oliver Horn's total life span had been begrudgingly condensed—like an hour candle burned through in a mere five minutes. Anything else would have resulted in his flame flickering out.

"......"

In exchange for this power, he'd lost a *lot* of future. Fully aware of that, Oliver decided he didn't care. This was the smallest of the prices he had to pay. Nothing compared to the *other* lives he was to cast upon the pyre.

"Heyyyyyy! OOOOOOliverrrrrr!"

His quiet reflections were shattered by a bellowing voice rushing toward him. Flinching, he turned and saw another boy climbing the irminsul toward him. Oliver was still aghast when the interloper caught up.

"Whew, I made it! Damn, you're fast. I almost lost you!"

"...Mr. Leik," Oliver said, reluctant to believe his eyes.

Yuri Leik, the self-proclaimed transfer student, was breathing heavily, grinning back at him. The cast around his torn-off limb was already gone. As soon as he caught his breath, he slapped Oliver on the shoulder.

"Please, call me Yuri! Man, this feels amazing! My fifth try, and I finally made it to the top! Ahhhh...that's the stuff."

His eyes swept the view, and he threw his arms out wide. His profile looked so unguarded, Oliver found himself making conversation.

"...You just kept hitting this layer? Even after losing an arm?"

"Well, yeah. I mean, I said I would! I dunno about anyone else, but if there's places I haven't been yet, I gotta check 'em out!"

This boy had the soul of an explorer.

"I'm glad you're here," he said, turning to Oliver. "This kind of triumph is best shared."

"_____"

It was so utterly guileless, it left Oliver speechless. Yuri's eyes were eagerly drinking in the view. The joy of a new discovery, his heart dancing at the sights before him—signs of an open, carefree mind. And all with a purity nigh impossible to perform.

Perhaps this boy had *no* ulterior motives. Oliver's gut told him so, despite all arguments to the contrary. His rational mind objected, and these two conclusions clashed within—and as a result, he chose to learn more.

"...Mr. Leik, are you—?"

"Ahhhhhhhhhhhh!"

But Yuri's shout drowned out his question. The transfer student darted off, bent over, and came back holding a bug in his hand. He proudly showed it to Oliver.

"Look, Oliver! I found a bug! This thing is so cool!"

"Don't pick it up if you don't know what it is! There's no telling what it'll do to you! Throw it—"

Oliver broke off mid-sentence. A wave of hostility had hit them, and only that mattered now.

He drew his athame, suddenly on guard. Yuri glanced around, bug in hand.

"Uh, Oliver...are we, like...surrounded?"

"...We clearly are. I probably should have stopped you. This isn't exactly a place for tourism," Oliver said. "But I didn't expect *this*. The peak here is kind of a buffer between the different beasts' domains. Normally, you never encounter any large magifauna here—much less find yourself under attack."

This could be a real problem. He alone could easily break through the pack and get away, but Yuri was still new to this layer, and bringing him along made things far more difficult. Plus, he was just starting to warm up to the boy, so he was disinclined to ditch him.

"Seems they're leaving us no choice... Can you fight, Mr. Leik?"

"Of course! There's a first time for everything!"

"You've never fought before?!" Oliver yelped, hoping like hell that was a joke.

Yuri just grinned at him. "Don't worry! What I don't know, I can pick up by *watching*."

He pulled a weapon from his scabbard. A rod with an edge—a construction far too simplistic to even call an athame.

"GYYYYYYYYYYYY!"

And a beast burst out of the brush, bound for Yuri. A midsize monkey. Light on its feet, it darted around Yuri, planted its hands on the ground like a somersault, and grabbed him with its prehensile toes. Yuri leaped back, dodging, looking very impressed.

"Wow, your feet are as strong as your hands!" he exclaimed.

As he made his observations, Oliver was firing a spell at a new assailant. The bulk of the troupe seemed focused on Yuri, easing his burden. While the transfer student's unpredictable behavior kept them confused, Oliver was steadily thinning their numbers.

"Getting a good grip down below would be so useful! My toes are shorter, but I wonder if I can do the same thing!"

Yuri might be fending off multiple foes at once, but he sure didn't sound like it. Intrigued by the monkeys' movements, he was actually trying to imitate them himself. He used spatial magic to make his soles stick to the ground, then manipulated his internal gravity to bend over backward.

"Oh, it worked! Look, I'm just like you! Monkey see, monkey do!"

"GYYYYYYYYYYYYYYYYY!"

One monkey seemed to take this as an affront and came charging at him. Still bent way over backward, Yuri put his hands on the ground and used them as an axis for an overhead kick, taking the monkey down. Oliver just gaped at him. Not the most logical way to fight, but the fact that it had worked at all spoke volumes to his natural talent.

They'd downed eight monkeys now, and the remaining beasts turned their backs and began retreating. Yuri looked surprised.

"Oh, they're running? They still had numbers!"

"No creatures fight to extinction. I'm more surprised they stuck around long enough to lose a third of their troupe. It's not like it's mating season…"

Oliver sheathed his athame, frowning. But a second later, Yuri's free hand clamped down on his shoulder.

"I knew I could count on you, Oliver."

"…Your point being?"

"What say we stick together? I've come this far. I'd like to see the fabled Battle of Hell's Armies."

He made this suggestion with no compunction—and even threw in a thumbs-up. Oliver couldn't believe pressing forward was even in the cards. Nonetheless—he was disinclined to refuse. The boy could clearly handle himself, but not to the extent that Oliver felt comfortable abandoning him.

"…I've already made it through. I can watch over your attempt, if that'll suffice?"

"It will! Just you wait—I'll get it in one!"

Yuri ran off, beaming with glee. Oliver turned to follow, and a thought struck him—the way this boy knew little of the world yet had the talent to overcome that, the way he just kept stepping closer even if you pushed him back… He was more than a bit like Nanao.

Amid the swirling schemes and conflicts in its midst, the broom league was making steady progress.

Chela and Miligan were in the stands watching a match featuring the Snake-Eyed Witch's main rival for the presidency—Percival Whalley. He had not given an inch in five clashes and had just downed his opponent.

"…Your opposition is rather good."

"Yes." Miligan nodded. "I'm certainly no match for him on a broom. Were it not for Nanao, he might even be the senior league's brightest young star."

She watched as he flew a slow loop, waving at the stands, then snorted.

"He's a thorn in my side but will probably make a good rival for Nanao. Just…I do rather hope she downs him. Their battle could well have a significant impact on the election."

She was never one to hide her motivations. As Whalley flew off, her eyes turned to the next contestant—the Empress of the broom, twelve matches in without a single loss.

"But clearly winning the league itself would be asking too much...
Ms. Ashbury is in a league of her own."

"Ashbury winning like this is less than ideal."

That same evening, in the old council's first-layer base, Leoncio was
growling at his followers.

"She has no interest in elections. She won't voice support for anyone
if she wins; in fact, she has a history of blowing off the speech entirely.
And all anyone will be talking about is how she trounced everybody.
Most vexing."

He shook his head. Whalley gritted his teeth, then put a hand to his
chest and stepped forward.

"...I *will* down her. If I win, then no problems—"

Leoncio had a death grip on his skull before he could finish. Watching the fear on his junior's face, he hissed, "That competitive spirit is
an advantage. But you expect me to *count* on it?"

"......!"

"...Hmph. Don't be petulant, Percy. The moment Ashbury chose
to enter, we all knew your odds of victory faded. This outcome is
expected. And we will not blame you for losing to her."

With that, he released Whalley, who was forced into an embittered
silence. Leoncio fixed him with a steely glare.

"That said—you *must* defeat Nanao Hibiya. That second-year girl is
supporting Miligan. And she has many eyes on her—if she steals the
show here, the ripple effects will hit the election hard," Leoncio cau-
tioned. "Your purpose in this league is to take her down a peg. Etch
that into your heart."

His tone brooked no argument, and Whalley took a knee in
acknowledgment. The rest was in his hands—yet Leoncio had his
hand to his chin, considering an alternate solution.

"That said, it's hardly fair for us to be sitting around fretting about
it. Don't you agree, Khiirgi?"

His gaze turned to the elf by the wall. He offered no specifics—but Avarice took the hint. A smile flickered across her eyes, dark as the hollow of an ancient tree.

They came for her on the path back to the dorms from late-night practice—when a broomrider who trained longer and harder than anyone else would be all on her own.

"…One on the right, two on the left, one above," Ashbury muttered, stopping below the arch over the path to the dorms. The darkness around her shimmered, returning no sound.

"I can hear *grass* breathing these days. Wriggle on out here, grubs."

She drew her athame, and spells emerged from the darkness in all three directions. The aim and timing were designed to give her no escape—yet they caught only air. The broom in her left hand had yanked her to the side.

"*Tonitrus.*"

Her return fire flushed an assailant out of the darkness. The attacker came rolling to their feet, aiming again—but Ashbury had broken into a run the moment her chant ended, moving ahead of them, her athame slicing across her foe's wrist.

Their hand was left dangling by the skin alone, their athame clattering on the ground. As the three remaining assailants gaped in horror, Ashbury wheeled toward them.

"…You move so slow, I got time to *yawn*. We done here? Then good night."

She rolled her eyes, and the shadows grew incensed. They leaped back, gaining distance from her. Abandoning the iron rule of nighttime attacks—keep the spell volume and power down to avoid unwanted attention—their voices chanted as one.

""""*Frigus Intensum!*""""

"*Ignis!*"

Flames flew over Ashbury's shoulder, far greater than the first spell's combined might, shielding her from their blizzard's gust.

"Morg—"

The flames struck a chord in her mind, and she spun around. Her eyes searched for a big man's face, that confident grin of old—though she knew it was in vain.

And her hopes were soon dashed. The man behind her was every bit as tall—but clearly not Morgan.

"Attacks on campus are not allowed. State your names and years!"

There stood the student body president, Alvin Godfrey, his voice ripe with fury. The three shadows turned tail and fled. No use lingering— this man's arrival meant their ambush had failed.

Godfrey made no effort to pursue. He merely glared after them.

"...Not giving chase?" Ashbury asked, raising a brow.

"I'd love to, but getting you back to the dorms intact is my priority here, Ms. Ashbury."

"I don't need your help."

"You're getting it anyway."

He was clearly insistent on that, and she knew him well enough to know no further argument would get her anywhere. She put her blade away and moved toward him.

As they walked side by side down the path to the dorms, she suddenly put two and two together.

"Ohhhh, it's election season. Was this part of that mess?"

"You fought them off unawares?"

"What do I care? No skin off my teeth. But if they're after me, then I guess they've got a candidate in the league?"

"...Candidates have entered. But I can't say for sure this is connected," he said grimly.

It was easy to make assumptions, but since he was backing a candidate himself—voicing those speculations carelessly could be deemed improper. That thought sealed his tongue. Ashbury was never the best at gleaning intent, but this much she could manage, and his straight-shooting style left her shaking her head.

"You haven't changed, then. Always were a meathead. Probably why you got along with him."

"...Morgan?"

There was a sad smile on his lips. Ashbury's old catcher had been a good friend to him as well.

"Those were the days. He gave me a lot of tips on controlling fire. Without him, I'd still be burning my own arms with every spell."

"He's good at handling threats. Be it fire or beast."

"...Hmm."

Godfrey was scratching his face thoughtfully. Ashbury shot him a baleful glare.

"...And I'm one of those?" she snapped.

"Y-you read my mind?! Since when can you—?!"

"It doesn't take magic to tell what's on a dipshit's mind. Context! Countenances! Creepy pauses!"

This man was an appalling actor. But even as she shuddered, a thought struck her, and she stopped in her tracks.

"Wait, speaking of dipshits—if these are election hijinks, then should you be shooting the shit here? There's someone with a bigger target on her back than mine."

Godfrey stopped dead. He wasn't *that* dumb.

"...Nanao Hibiya? They might go for it, but she'll be fine. I've got other Watch eyes on her. And she's not prone to late-night solo pract—"

"That's assuming she heads back to the dorms after practice. You really think the leagues would be enough to make her turn in early? She's every bit as dumb as you."

Ashbury took a step closer with every line, and Godfrey's expression turned grim. He turned toward the school building.

"...Ms. Ashbury, I'll have to take my—"

"I said I didn't need help! Go on, get!"

Her roar on his heels, the man broke into a run. Few words hit harder than *"as dumb as you."* If that was true, there was no way she would cooperate.

Meanwhile, amid the teeming life of the bustling forest, beneath the everlasting artificial sun, Oliver was once more at the base of the irminsul for rehab—and shaking his head.

"…You again, Mr. Leik."

"I've been waiting for *you*, Oliver!"

He let out the loudest sigh he could muster. But Yuri was not discouraged, and he came dashing over, grinning merrily. Oliver kept a few steps back, on guard.

"…I don't remember ever agreeing to meet you at the base of the irminsul. Did you spot me coming from up above and dash down to meet me?"

"Oh, you noticed?! That's right! I've just been hanging out up there. Resting a while, taking in the view—then I saw you coming and was like, I just gotta!"

"What a fortuitous coincidence!"

Yuri's excitable yammer was interrupted by a new voice as someone else landed behind him. Oliver realized who she was and nearly jumped out of his skin.

"…Nanao?! Why are *you* here?! Where did you even come from?!"

"Like this gentleman here, I was lying in wait atop yonder tree. You have neglected to invite me on your labyrinth excursions of late."

"Because things are dangerous right now, and I told you to stay on the surface!" Oliver yelled, advancing on her. "You're in the league! And everyone knows you're on the current council's side. There's danger even on campus, and you come sauntering down into the wilds of the labyrinth—what if someone attacked?!"

"Fair points, all," she said, hanging her head.

That was when Yuri smacked a fist on his palm and stepped in between them.

"I think that's just about enough, Oliver. Lots of light on this layer and plenty of people around. And since voices carry on the air, it's probably safer than the first layer."

"You stay out of this, Mr. Leik. This is between—"

"Calm down, Oliver. Deep breaths."

When he tried to speak again, Yuri pulled him away from her, over by a root. Then he jerked a thumb back at Nanao.

"See that face? She knew all along what you're saying is true. And she came anyway."

"? That's worse! Why take the risk—?"

"Obviously. She just wuvs you so, so, so, so, so, so, so, so, so, so, so, so, so, so, so, so, so, so, so, soooo much! She came to see *you*! She couldn't wait till tomorrow! She needed to be with you so bad, she didn't even factor in the risks!"

Yuri was shaking Oliver's shoulders now, getting rather worked up himself. But Nanao was far enough away that she couldn't make out what they were saying.

Head down, she murmured, "...I just wished to be with you, Oliver."

And that struck Oliver like an arrow to the heart. It took his breath away. He had to clear his throat several times before turning back to her.

"...Well, acting in haste will just draw attention. Let's head back up carefully, making sure we don't run into any sketchy characters," he told her. "There are lights in the lounges and study groups burning the midnight oil—far less risk of ambush than here. If you wish, we can sit and talk awhile. How does that sound, Nanao?"

Her face lit up.

Yuri gave them a satisfied nod, then said, "I've had enough exploring for one day. Much as I'd love to give you two some room, best we stick together until we reach the surface, yes? Safety in numbers."

"...Can't argue with that. Very well, Mr. Leik... Honestly, your delving this deep not long after your transfer here is pretty risky, too."

"Don't worry! From now on, I'll only delve with you, Oliver! Sound good, Nanao?"

"Verily! I believe we shall be firm friends."

Nanao and Yuri exchanged high fives. Oliver rubbed his temples. He'd sensed they had some common ground, personality-wise—and clearly, he'd been right.

Now he had to look after *two* unruly children. Sighing, he turned to head back up…but stopped a step later.

"…Wait." There was an urgency to his tone that cut their cheery introductions short. Eyes on the dense vegetation before them, feeling the hostility within, Oliver muttered, "Too late."

Then he turned on his heel, breaking into a run. He grabbed both companions' wrists, pulling them along, and they soon followed suit, each keeping an eye on their backs. Chants echoed behind.

"…Oliver!"

"Oliver!"

"Up the tree!"

The ground at their feet and the brush to one side were struck by bolt after bolt. Narrowly avoiding the storm through serpentine footwork, they made it back to the base of the irminsul and started up a branch.

Not far along it was a large burl, and they dove behind it, taking cover. An instant later, an especially large lightning bolt struck the other side. Oliver let out a breath.

"…Okay, we've got the positional advantage. They can't flank us or hit us from behind without a lengthy detour around the branches, and if they're sticking to the shrubbery, they can't get too close. If they take to their brooms and fly up, we can shoot them down before they get close."

Even as he spoke, his mind was on something else. If he didn't catch her mana frequency here, then Teresa was out of range. She'd warned him as much; she'd be out today, helping with a scheme to turn the faculty on one another. His comrades weren't coming to help—the three of them would have to escape this together.

"Keep one eye out for flanking maneuvers and hit them hard if you catch a glimpse. Don't miss your chance."

Both nodded. Yuri was peering over the rim at the brush below.

"...Five of 'em," he said. "Two upperclassmen."

"You can see them?"

"No, but I asked. Oh, here comes one. **Flamma**."

He waved his athame. A moment later, an enemy stepped out of the brush, right into Yuri's spell.

"Gah...!"

"See?" Yuri grinned.

Oliver attempted a follow-up, but this was neutralized by a different foe's support barrage, and he was forced back behind the burl. The damaged foe dove into the shrubbery. To Oliver's eye, they were moving a little slower. He turned to Yuri.

"Mm? What's up, Oliver? Something on my face?"

A smile as clear as the sun. *But how did he—?*

Before he could finish that thought, the enemy's explosion spell struck the burl. He was forced to shoot back. The enemy was trading suppressing fire, curving spells across cover, trying to get a bead on them. Oliver threw up barrier spells on their flanks, returning fire.

"**Fragor!** No, keep doing what you're doing. Can't let them get close."

"Hrm, there is precious little I can contribute in a fight of this nature."

"That's not true. Even if you're just firing at random, it helps. What matters isn't hitting them but making it clear a careless move will get them hit."

"That, I can manage, but will we not start a fire?"

"Damage to the forest itself will be repaired by the labyrinth homeostasis. Unless you're Godfrey, there's no risk of turning this place into scorched earth. Go for broke."

That freed Nanao from all concern, and she took a swing with her katana.

"Very well. *Flamma!*"

Polished by her mind's eye, a fireball flew from the tip of her blade. It landed in a corner of a copse and burst, lighting up the terrain for yards in every direction. An enemy happened to be lurking near and was forced to dive out of the line of fire—not missing a beat, Oliver downed them with a follow-up spell.

"Wow, Nanao!" Yuri yelled. "You burned all that with a singlecant?"

"I've begun to find the knack for it, yes."

"With your mana output, that's the kind of force you *should* be casting," Oliver murmured. "They know we're second-years, so they'll have assumed we can't hit that hard—it was a real stroke of luck we managed to down one."

He glanced toward the unmoving foe by the burning copse. He'd hit them with decent force—they weren't getting back up soon, even if a friend healed them. And if Yuri was right, there were four more.

"It's going well!" Yuri said. "Seems like they can't get up here—have we got this in the bag?"

"Absolutely not. At least, if you're right about the two upperclassmen."

Oliver was disinclined to be optimistic. Fighting Vera Miligan his first year had knocked that out of him. At Kimberly, "upperclassmen" meant fourth-year and above—so two of their remaining foes were Miligan-level or worse.

"…It's only gonna get tougher. Here they come!"

He spotted two figures breaking out of the brush. Their footwork was too nimble, their speed too fast—they *had* to be the upperclassmen.

"Aim for the leader!"

At Oliver's word, all three focused their spells. If they split their fire, both might get through; it was best to make sure they took down one at a time. They were on a long, thin irminsul branch—only one way up to them. Taking full advantage of that terrain, they might have a shot at downing them this way—but Oliver knew only too well that was a faint hope.

"……!"

His worst fears were realized. As they reached the branch, the approaching figures shifted to the side—and the *underside*. Racing up the branch using Wall Walk—but of course they did. Any sword arts technique Oliver and Nanao had mastered was old hat to an upperclassman.

"Do it, Nanao!"

He *had* anticipated this, and it was *why* he'd chosen this spot to camp. Even as he shouted the order, he grabbed Yuri's hand, pulling him back, gesturing at the bark below with his athame. Nanao saw that—and knew exactly what he wanted.

"At once! *Gladio!*"

She swung her blade down. A full-strength severing spell directed at the branch below them—and cut it through.

"——?!"

"……!"

No longer connected, the branch creaked, then began to fall. Both assailants let out silent yelps. A branch of the irminsul was the size of a fully grown tree, and second-years could use only single incantations— no one would expect them to manage *this* feat. They had yet to fully grasp how exceptional Nanao really was.

But this in no way ended the fight. One foe went down with the branch, fleeing to the surface. But the figure at the fore kept right on running, never slowing down. As she approached the schism, she worked their way back to the top and jumped. The gap was a good twelve yards wide—too far to vault. She put her hand on her broom, trying to propel herself across, but—

""""Impetus!"""""

Three gale spells were waiting for that. Their foe threw out the oppo- sitional element, but channeling mana into her broom while countering three spells at once was a bit much even for an upperclassman. Enough wind got past to slow her down—and she released the broom. In the air, she was a sitting duck—dropping to the ground was the only escape. Oliver was certain they had her, but—

"Haaa-ha!"

A breathy laugh sent shudders down their spines. Their foe did *not* fall—instead, she stepped onto the air, jumping. *Twice.*

"___?!"

None of them had expected *this.* The second jump took her beneath them, putting the branch between her and their spells. She snagged a protrusion, flipping herself upside down and planting her feet on the underside of the branch. Then she came walking *around* it toward the top.

"......!"

All three of them backed down the branch, keeping their distance, but this time, Oliver genuinely couldn't believe it. Sky Walk—and *two* steps. Even *one* required incredible talent and massive amounts of training. If she could take *two* steps, she was a master of the form. It was a feat far beyond even Miligan's caliber.

They clearly weren't dealing with an ordinary upperclassman here. This had to be one of the top fighters in the upper years. Her uniform disguised the specific year, but Oliver looked her over again, searching for clues. She had a hood deep over an ancient wood-carved mask, hiding her face from view.

"...Don't suppose you'd care to share your name?" he asked, allowing a touch of spite.

His mind was churning. She hadn't used a doublecant, probably concerned the scale of the ensuing spell would attract attention. Even at this hour, there were plenty of students on the second layer, including Campus Watch members. He could bet on that and cast a siren spell or toss out a rescue orb, but...

"Not yet the time for that, Oliver," Nanao said, catching his thought. She flashed a grin, and it hit him like a bolt from the blue. He caught a whiff of his own timidity buried beneath the workings of his rational mind.

"…Right you are, Nanao."

He nodded, raising his athame to midstance. That bet would have been presumptuous. No guarantee a call for help would improve the situation; it might well drag in an even bigger threat. It was a last resort when nothing else could be done—but things were not yet that dire.

"…Come on, then. It's high time I stopped quaking in my boots whenever I face an upperclassman."

His words were half a whip across his flagging spirits. Their strategy *had* paid off—they'd managed to turn this into a three-on-one fight for the moment. That was a solid advantage and one they'd *earned*. Now they simply had to follow through on it.

"Turbo Flamma!"

As if extolling Oliver's courage, a flaming tornado kicked up behind their foe.

"You're really going at it. Mind if I join in?"

A low growl—not a voice you'd ever mistake. As the flames died down, all eyes turned toward the man on the ground—the three of them, the foe before them, and the enemy attempting the long way around.

"Morgan!" Nanao cried.

Clifton Morgan raised a hand in acknowledgment, taking in the scene.

"Hmmmm? …Am I imagining things, or do you have *two* upperclassmen?" he said. "Gah-ha-ha! I must be! That'd be an absolute disgrace! At your age, ganging up on three second-year kids."

His assessment had certainly brought out the sarcasm. And with literal sparks flying from every inch of him, his words packed a real punch.

"That would be intolerable. If it were true, I'd have to *clean up*. With a *charcoal* filter."

With that, he raised his athame high. The girl before them clicked her tongue, then flung herself off the branch, landing in the brush below. The others beat a hasty retreat in kind, vanishing into the forest. When there was no trace of them left, Morgan finally lowered his blade.

"They're gone. Gah-ha! You kids never learn," Morgan said, glancing up the irminsul at them. "Delving at a time like this? I guess that is pretty dang Kimberly of you."

The three of them jumped down, Nanao at the fore.

"The assistance was most appreciated, Morgan," she said. "And timely, as I have need to speak with you. Can you spare a moment?"

Morgan cocked an eyebrow. And Oliver realized Nanao was not *just* here to see him—she had bigger fish to fry.

Attack Nanao Hibiya in the labyrinth with lasting damage, be it wounds or a curse. No need to fell her, just prevent her from flying at peak performance. That was how she'd interpreted Leoncio's intent.

After all, the girl was a second-year, and the task itself was far too easy for *her*. And it was inherently in bad taste. Even Kimberly students had an unwritten understanding that fights were best left to those of similar ages. For that reason, she had not planned on being directly involved—the plan had been to kick back and watch her juniors take care of business.

"…Haaa-ha-ha!"

The memory brought a smirk to her lips. She hadn't expected to have *such fun.*

Leaning against the wall, the masked woman's gasping sigh of a laugh pealed on and on. The male student across from her intensified his glare.

"…What's so funny? You *failed* miserably."

He didn't even try to hide his frustration. They were in one of the old council's bases on the first layer, and their candidate, Percival Whalley, was biting his nails again. The cause of his irritation was none other than the report from the failed ambush team.

"The targets showed such promise, you let them see you Sky Walk? *Both* steps?! Far too rash. Why even bother hiding your ears and face?!"

At Whalley's howl, Barman shrugged. He'd been behind the counter, silently working a shaker.

"I agree, but it's hardly unprecedented. How long have you known this covetous elf?"

"Yes, her lusts are much too unfettered! Why were you even *at* the scene? It was hardly a plan we could not afford to fail. Do you have no concept of risk and reward?"

Whalley glared at her again. His strategies were always constructed of the purest logic, and he frequently found the whims of his allies a far greater threat than anything an enemy could do.

But despite the scathing rebuke, the ambush leader removed her hood and mask with a smile. The sixth-year elf—Khiirgi.

"…I only meant to sneak a peek. Kill some time. Then I saw how they fought, and the itch took hold. Like being out for a walk and seeing a young doe shaking her tail at you. How could I *not* play?"

Avarice showed no remorse. As Whalley fumed further, she took a quiet step toward him, cupping his ruddy cheeks in her hands.

"Don't you scowl at me, Percy. If there are consequences, *I'll* handle them. This will *not* stop you from winning the election. Besides, we reeled in some better news. Right, Leoncio?"

Khiirgi's head swiveled. At the back of the room, a man sat deep in a chair.

"Indeed," he said, nodding. "Morgan—you're *alive*."

His hand clutched a crystal. Inside, images and voices played—a hearty laugh, delivered by a confident man. A sixth-year student all had assumed long since consumed by the spell.

Kimberly generally held two leagues for broomsports a year. They'd hold leagues for all three disciplines, and once those were done, the second league would loop back through the disciplines in the same order. The order of those disciplines varied by year, but this year it was broom fights, then broom wars, and finally broom races.

"The white-hot fury of the broom fight's first league wrapped up yesterday! Missing them already? Don't you worry—the next party's already starting! Broom wars league one starts todaaaaaaaaay!"

To many mages, broomsports were synonymous with broom wars. The stands were filled to the brim, and the crowd was already roaring. Roger had to raise his voice to be heard above everyone.

"One-on-one is fun, but this here is the main event! Not just raw player talent—wars require strategies and teamwork, too! An extra heaping of everything good—like your plate at the end of the buffet line. Where do you even begin, Instructor Dustin?"

"I promise you, he isn't kidding. *There's too much going on! I don't even know where to look!* That's what everyone says the first time they watch the broom wars. It's more than enough to just keep your eyes on a favorite player, so don't think *too* hard about it—but it is true that learning how to watch a game will enhance your enjoyment. I thought I'd explain a few tricks for you all today."

"Please do! Our first round is the Rabid Hawks versus the Blue Swallows! Come on out, O beloved brutal broomriderrrrrs!"

The horns blared, and from east and west, two teams shot onto the field. The Blue Swallows were on the east, doing their final pre-match rundowns.

"...Uh, Ashbury, I should at least ask."

"I'll do my thing. You keep up as best you can."

She didn't even bother glancing his way. A chorus of sighs went up from the team.

"Our ace never minces words."

"Can't argue with results, though."

"With the streak you've been on, any strategy would just tie your hands anyway."

There were definitely some sour grapes here, but Ashbury just took them all as statements of fact, grinning like a shark.

"You know it. I'll down 'em all in the first half. It's time I had a perfect match."

"Madness!"

"But those eyes—she means it!"

"I'm too scared to look her in the eye!"

When their ace spoke, all shuddered. And the horns sounded again, forcing them onto the field.

Both teams sprang into action. As the breathless crowd cheered, Roger slapped the table.

"And they're off! Ohhh boy! My eyes already can't keep up! Where should I look, Instructor?"

"Don't try to focus on a single point. Take in the whole field. Observe how the players are arranged around their captains—that'll give you a solid sense of what each team's plan of action is. The Rabid Hawks are making it easy for you—they're in a standard formation, balancing offense and defense."

Dustin's tone was almost talking the announcer down. Naturally, Roger hadn't gotten this job without being a longtime broomsports fan—he knew exactly how to watch a match without any tutorials. But it was his style to act like a newbie fan when the need arose. Just as he had in the broom fights, he carefully played along with the broom teacher's lessons.

"A broomrider without speed is helpless. This isn't like chess—you can't leave your king sitting pretty. You see what they do instead?"

"I do! That's why both captains are doing loops on the far ends of the field!"

Roger pointed a finger in each direction. Like he said, both captains were maintaining speed, but not leaving the narrow confines of their team's territory.

"Right you are," Dustin said with a nod. "With two guards on each. Naturally, if the enemy flies their way, the attack squads'll knock 'em down. I'm sure everyone's gut tells 'em this much, but in broom wars, it's never easier to down a player than when they're busy chasing someone else. The captain is the biggest target and the player they can least afford to lose—yet at the same time, they serve to draw the offense's attention. It's a role that requires nerves of steel."

Dustin flashed a shit-eating grin. Broom wars was a sport demanding constant action, and a captain who just hung out at the back was doing nobody any good. When the other team was on the run, the captain would be chasing, too; when their side was on the run, the captain would be fighting back. That's how the game was played.

"The other roles are also aptitude-based. Aggressive, fearless types get sent first into the fray; cautious, defensive types are tasked with fending off the enemy's assaults. But those role divisions are always in flux. If the situation demands it, the whole team can go on the offense—it's what we call the Full Attack formation. You'll most likely see it in the back half of the match, once one side has a big numbers advantage."

"And until that happens, both sides are trying to thin each other out."

"Yep. At the start, the attackers are going at each other, while the back line watches for their chance to swoop in and help. Basically, those frontline fights are the main thing to watch in the early going. Unlike broom fights, they get hit from the side all the time, so nothing is ever predictable. A single downed player can shake up the whole game."

Even as he spoke, the two teams' attackers were clashing—and then a player shot through the center of the fight, rocketing toward the opposition's rear line. The crowd gasped.

"Whoa, Ashbury's going in solo? Instructor, is that allowed?"

"...Oh, she's starting already? I mean, it's normally not a good idea. That's the problem with her matches. 'Normal' really doesn't apply," said Dustin. "I mentioned how the captain's job is to bait the opposition? Same goes for small squads flying deep into the enemy zone. Nobody's about to just let 'em be. They can monopolize their foe's attention and create gaps in the enemy lines that their teammates can take advantage of."

He sounded annoyed—or was *pretending* to be—but there was definitely a hint of a stifled laugh behind it. He knew full well the risks but couldn't help himself. Every broom wars fan loved to see a single player tear up the rules.

Fighting the temptation to abandon his commentator role and act like a regular old fan, clinging to the illusion of being a proper instructor, Dustin managed, "It's a batshit crazy position only the dumbest and best can pull off. We call it…the berserker."

He wasn't wrong. The moment Ashbury flew in, it became impossible for the Rabid Hawks to think straight.

"Guh!"

"Gaughhh—!"

She hit a player's back in passing, and they plummeted. A teammate swooping in to retaliate crashed into another player in pursuit. As they tried to regain their balance, Ashbury flitted back and finished them off. Panic spread among the rest of the Hawks. This was no time to stick to their positions—everyone made their own best judgments, going after Ashbury. All cohesion lost, chaos reared its head.

"Wait up, damn it!"

"How long are you gonna keep this up?!"

But the harder they tried to put her down fast, the more they danced in the palm of Ashbury's hand. She stirred up their formation, leaving the Rabid Hawks in disarray, and the Blue Swallows' offense was mercilessly taking advantage of that. Once the collapse began, there was no stopping it. Hawk after Hawk went down; Ashbury slipped past club after club swung her way, grinning like a maniac.

"Isn't it obvious? Till every last one of you is down!"

*   *   *

The audience gulped as one. This wasn't a match. It was a *hunt*.

Normally, berserkers didn't stay flying for long. Flying solo into the heart of enemy territory made it all the more likely you'd be downed quick. Create a minute of chaos and let your team handle the rest— that was more than enough. But Ashbury *wasn't going down*. In fact, she was dropping her foes left and right.

"…As a broomrider, Ashbury's physique and skills are both beyond perfection."

This wasn't even commentary anymore. Dustin had actually cut the voice amp spell and was just talking to himself, unable to peel his eyes off Ashbury. Next to him, Roger could only listen.

"Even to *my* eyes. She's always been far more a pure rider than I ever was. My job was to cut down the monsters on the front lines of the Gnostic hunts, but she's only ever had one enemy—time. I honed my speed so I could kill faster. In the back of my mind, speed itself was never more than a means to an end. But not with her. Speed *is* the goal, and her entire life is devoted to that pursuit. She's never once wavered from that."

Dustin spoke with a mixture of awe and envy. Then he said a number aloud.

"2:25:21. You know what that number is?"

"…Every broomsports fan knows that number, Instructor."

"That they do. The infamous world record for the broom race regulation course."

The broomriding instructor spoke as if beholding a marvel.

"That's what Ashbury's really up against. Can she surpass that number? That's the sole meaning of her life. But the rider who set that record died even as they shattered it. It's one of *those* numbers. The time itself is a *spell*."

"…The time…is a spell…"

"There's one other reason I said time is her enemy. Broomriders pushing the limits of speed hit the peak of their abilities shockingly early. Late teens, early twenties. Past that point, your times at the highest speeds stop improving. There are a lot of theories why—but I say you just accumulate too much other stuff." Dustin went on. "Ashbury is twenty years old. The hard limit on setting that record is coming up fast. She knows that better than anyone."

From the way she was running the field wild, Dustin could *feel* her urgency. Yet, another part of him sensed he could never truly *know* what it felt like. Like that former top player once said, riders aiming to be the world's fastest were always alone. And no coach could do anything to help.

"I'll say it again—Ashbury's techniques are flawless. It's only her mind holding her back. And she's using the broom fights and broom wars to amp up her competitiveness, trying to get herself where she needs to be. It may look like madness. But there are some barriers you can't bust down unless you're crazy."

Every student watching Ashbury fly *knew*. Her way of living was how a mage ought to be. And it made them ask themselves—could they even be that insanely committed to their own goals?

"I dunno if the attempt'll bear fruit. But I can say one thing for sure: I'm a fan. Always have been, am right now—and always will be."

Dustin said no more. He just watched his student fly like any rider dreamed of. So far, so bright—as if she were burning her light into his eyes before it went out for good.

Just as promised, she'd wiped out the entire team—and like always, Ashbury skipped the post-match meeting, not even changing out of her uniform. She was stalking across the campus, still trailing her mid-match intensity with her. Students she passed flinched and kept their distance, as if spotting a wounded beast.

"...*Huff... Huff...!*"

She made it to the fountain and plunged her whole head in. Too drastic to really call a cooldown—this was more like a blacksmith cooling heated metal. Her body and mind were too revved up, and nothing else would do the trick.

As she pulled her head out of the water, she heard a man's voice.

"…Your ferocity scalds the very eye," he said.

Golden locks reflected in the rippling water. She'd known he was there and didn't bother turning around.

"I don't give a warg shit about the election. Do whatever the hell you want."

"We fully intend to. But there is one thing I thought you should know."

Leoncio took a step up beside her, placing a crystal on the rim of the fountain. The image contained within began to play, along with a certain voice. A timbre she would never mistake.

"Proof—that Clifton Morgan is still alive."

Time froze around her. Taking that as the response he'd hoped for, Leoncio turned to leave.

"Keep it," he said. "You can easily prove the authenticity. That's all I ask for. I'll be cheering for you, Ashbury."

With that transparent falsehood, he sailed away. Ashbury never once looked at him. Her eyes stayed locked on the crystal's contents.

That evening, the Wild Geese were holding an emergency meeting to discuss the outcome of the league's first game.

"The Blue Swallows are *trouble*," Melissa said, grimly scanning the faces of her teammates. She was essentially speaking for everyone here; there was no need to drive home the urgency of the situation. "Or at least—Ashbury is. She shot right into the heart of the enemy and downed six all on her own. That's just messed up ! *No one* can do that!"

"I could scarcely believe my own eyes. Her triumphs are absolutely outstanding!"

Nanao was all smiles, not a trace of concern. She had the most unabashed respect for Ashbury here, and that wasn't wavering—a fact that earned her a lot of winces from her teammates. Melissa moved over, patted her on the head, and then went back to the fore.

"We try normal tactics, we'll be pulverized, too. We'll need to dig deep on formations, tactics, and roles. Ideas, anyone?"

Everyone looked lost in thought.

"…Well, really, if we can take out Ashbury—we win."

"Is 'go for the ace' an actual strategy, per se?"

"Nobody else has pulled it off."

"And Ashbury *wants* us all fixated on her."

"But letting her fly free is *worse*."

They weren't getting anywhere. Everyone had thoughts and plenty of enthusiasm, but the discussion lacked concrete details—so Oliver thought hard and raised a hand. The team captain, Hans Leisegang, spotted that at once.

"Speak, Horn."

"…What if we start at Full Attack?"

A buzz went through the room. It was like a rock heaved into a pond, and before the ripples could die down, Oliver spoke again.

"It's a drastic measure, but it eliminates the point of having a berserker. If there's no formation to disrupt, they're just another attacker. It boils things down to which side can drop the other captain first."

"…Abandon defense for an all-out brawl. It makes a certain kind of sense."

"But…that's still where Ashbury shines."

"Dismissing suggestions based on *that* would leave us with a big ol' pile of nothing."

"Is there anything she isn't great at?"

"Teamwork."

"Communication."

"Speaking for five seconds without winding someone up."

These last three were all at once, which got a big laugh, and Melissa smacked each speaker in turn. Hans had been lurking quietly at the back watching things over, but deeming it time, he chimed in.

"It's a good idea…but I'm against it."

Everyone went quiet, waiting for what came next. His tone level, the Wild Geese captain began to elaborate.

"Starting broom wars at Full Attack means abandoning the sport of it. It leaves us all just fending for ourselves. There's no 'team' left in it. If you ask me anyway."

Oliver straightened up. This was exactly the response he'd been hoping his suggestion would provoke.

"I'm not making some grand statement that a cohesive group can overcoming individual prowess. Mages all gotta rely on their own skills, after all. The Blue Swallows are getting results by letting their ace off the leash as we speak. Letting everyone else fly in the wake of their greatest talent—maybe that's even the ideal formation. But we Wild Geese do things differently. Right?"

Hans paused, looking each player in the eye in turn.

"We aren't as nuts as Ashbury, but we got plenty of trouble right here. Nobody listens to a word I say, and plans we make before the match frequently get thrown right out the second we start playing. Most of you will draw your wands the moment your opinions are in conflict. But even so, there's one thing we've all got in common. We're all here to *enjoy* flying."

He raised a clenched fist. His words rang true; that was the heart of everyone here.

"Players who focus only on the fun of the game are called hedonists. And the Wild Geese are chosen for their hedonism. You all know that. And you know that flying in sync with your team is more fun than doing whatever you please. You know the thrill of having all your roles working together like clockwork." He then added, "Once again, I don't think teamwork is *better* than individual skill. It's simply—we are all of us, together, a single giant goose. Big enough to swallow up some pissant little swallows, right?"

He flashed a grin, and Nanao's hand shot up.

"Fight not the enemy's strategy but utilize our own greatest strengths. Is that the essence of your speech, Commander?"

"Good phrasing, Hibiya. Our greatest strength is our passion for the *joys* of broom wars. And in light of that—does starting at Full Attack sound like *fun*? I bet we can think of something we'd *all* like better."

Oliver knew this had shifted the focus of the discussion. He need add nothing more himself—Hans had put it in plain language, and it had always been the team's alignment.

"Lemme add a rule to this debate. Don't plan how to win. Plan how to have *fun*." And then he finished with, "You all know why! That's the plan that'll bring out our best."

The meeting lasted a good four hours. When Oliver left the clubhouse and headed toward the arena, the skies were already dark. There, he found an upperclassman seated on the grass.

"...Captain."

"Mm? Oh, Horn," the man said, looking up. The Wild Geese captain had been in that same meeting with him. Their reunion was no coincidence—Oliver had come here specifically looking for him. Hans fired his famous broad grin over his shoulder. "Sorry about earlier. I kinda used your suggestion as a springboard."

"Not at all. I never expected that idea to go through."

He knew Hans knew that had always been the point of his proposal. Perhaps a bit too obliging of his teammate, Hans chuckled and turned his eyes back to the night sky.

"Honestly, if this was just one match in a normal league, I might have gone for it," he said. "It never hurts to try new things, and it could be a good chance to reevaluate everyone's offensive potential. That goes double when we stand little chance of winning otherwise. But the way Ashbury's playing? This is our one shot at going up against a rider like her. She's at her peak. She won't be like this next year."

Oliver nodded, saying not a word. This was something any mage could feel in their bones. Ashbury was *burning her life away*. It wouldn't last long, and there was no turning back. Oliver's own version of that might be different in nature, but he knew only too well how rough it was.

"I don't wanna waste our time flying with her on a strategy that ain't like us. Win or lose—I'm a hedonist all the way."

The captain smiled like a naughty child. Oliver laughed and sat down next to him.

"…I think that's what drew Nanao and me to this team."

"Aw, you're gonna make me cry!"

The captain's large hand mussed the boy's hair. Oliver winced but indulged Hans—his thoughts began turning to Nanao's role in the upcoming Blue Swallows match.

After the team spent three days running through every possible scenario, the big day arrived—it was one PM.

"Here it is! Day four of the broom wars league! The Wild Geese versus the Blue Swallows! The teams are streaming in from east and west!"

The announcer, Roger, was already going full bore. Watching the players take to the skies, he turned to Dustin once again seated by his side.

"Instructor, how do you see this going?"

"The Blue Swallows have already won two games playing a winning strategy. Ashbury rockets into the opponents' formation, causing chaos; then her team's attacks press that advantage, and once they've dropped a few and have momentum, they switch to Full Attack. Both matches were perfect victories, so there's no reason to think they'll change up that plan. It all hinges on how the Wild Geese plan to fight back."

The match itself would show what the two teams had in mind. The

Blue Swallows were hot right now, but could the Wild Geese nip that in the bud? That thought was on the mind of every audience member. And Blue Swallows fans were no exception. They loved to see their team win but still craved a good game. Two conflicting impulses that existed inside them all.

The horns sounded, heralding the start of the match. Both teams' attackers shot forward, and one Swallow peeled away from the pack. The start everyone had expected.

"And they're off! Ashbury already charging in, as she is wont to do! What now, Wild Geese? Got anything that can handle her ludicrous violence?"

"They're not using any unusual formations. I figured there was a chance they'd go for broke and start at Full Attack, but apparently not. Hopefully they've got something *else* in mind, but…"

Dustin had his arms folded, scowling at the Wild Geese. Ashbury had already slipped through their front line and was in full berserker mode: hitting anyone she got near, forcing all their attention onto her. Maneuvers so good, no sense or standards need apply.

"Ashbury's in their camp all alone, wrecking face! Same as the matches before! And her team's attackers are closing in! The Wild Geese are in trouble!"

"…They're not doing bad, actually," Dustin muttered. It might look like the same outcome, but he'd spotted a critical difference. "They're all keeping their wits about them. Ashbury's deep in their pocket—but *not* causing chaos."

Dustin's take was right on the money. The Wild Geese's strategy was already in full swing.

"Oh shit! Oh shiiiit!"

Ashbury was hot on the heels of a player known for using his tiny frame to make tight maneuvers, an asset when running from a faster foe—comparatively. But here, that just meant it took *slightly* longer for him to go down.

"You! Wait right there!" Melissa roared. She'd come in swinging, trying to prevent that fate. Every bit as experienced as the captain himself, her flying was notoriously stable—she excelled less at felling foes than avoiding getting felled herself. Enough that she could go a few rounds with Ashbury and live.

"…I'm up next, eh? Gotta get her after me, then. C'mon!"

The third player was also a veteran sixth-year. He was possibly an even better fit for this role than the other two. Ashbury had downed him more than another player at Kimberly—for one simple reason: *"I don't like the way he flies."*

"So that's three defenders on Ashbury."

The end of the earlier meeting. The Wild Geese captain had gone through all the opinions offered and settled on this plan.

"But let's be clear, their job is not to drop her—they're bait. They're trying to keep her attention on them. Specifically, the three of them will take turns *making* her chase them. The four of you will be playing a different game—and nobody else will pay Ashbury any attention unless she's directly coming after them. This should help limit the extent of her disruptive tactics."

This drew a series of *hmm*s. Everyone got the logic behind it, but…

"Make her chase us? That's tricky."

"By having three on Ashbury, we can minimize other casualties, right?"

"That's easier than dropping her, I guess."

"But how sustainable is it? She's gonna figure it out sooner or later."

"We're not saying keep it up indefinitely. This strategy is for the start of the match only. If you can keep her at it for four or five minutes, great. In light of that—do we have any volunteers?"

The captain looked around, and Nanao's hand shot up first.

"Let me at her!"

"Good answer, but…Hibiya, we've got another role for you."

That was all she needed to hear, and she sat back down. By the board, Melissa quietly raised a hand.

"…Then I'll go. I'm a good fit. I've gone up against her plenty."

There was a longer silence, and then other hands started going up.

"I'm probably right for it. She's chased me often enough that I've gotta pretty good idea of what'll piss her off."

"But we'll need variety in that department. I guess I could bring out her vicious streak…"

The captain grinned at his volunteers. Once again certain that the Wild Geese's greatest strength was their differences.

"Good work, all three of you," Hans muttered. They were getting the job done. They had a handful of minutes before Ashbury figured it out, and it was on him to put that to good use.

"Forward!"

He threw up a hand sign, and the players who saw it—attacker and defender alike—shot forward.

"…Whoa! That's a shocker. The Wild Geese have Ashbury deep in their zone, yet half the team's on the offensive!"

"Aha! So that's the gambit," Dustin crowed, leaning forward in his seat, his eyes glittering at the unexpected turn up above. "That's a problem for Ashbury. The rest of her team have been forced into defensive positions—her disrupting the back lines is accomplishing nothing."

The berserker's effectiveness depended on the opportunities they created for the rest of their team. But with everyone too busy defending to follow up on her moves, that meant she was stranded in enemy territory. A lost soldier with no effect on the war at hand.

It didn't take her long to work that out. Dustin saw her glance toward the far side of the field and muttered, "Yep, you've *gotta* turn back. But when you do…"

"…Tch—"

Realizing her actions were getting her team nowhere, Ashbury turned to head back to her side—but the instant her attention shifted away from the fight at hand, a club came swinging toward her from diagonally above.

"———?!"

She barely blocked it with her own weapon, but from a less-than-ideal posture—she failed to fully redirect the force of the hit. Knocked off balance, she lost speed and altitude while she righted herself. With far less momentum, she wheeled through the sky below, voices raining down on her.

"Going somewhere, Ashbury?"

"I'm insulted! You're dancing with *us*, remember?"

"That's right! You've yet to drop *anyone*."

The three players she'd been chasing. They'd cast off all pretense of being mere prey and were baring their talons—*after* stealing the height advantage.

Ashbury's lips twitched.

"Buzz off, gnats!"

"Ohhhhhhhhhh?! The Wild Geese trio going *hard*! The moment Ashbury tried to back up her side, they landed a good one! Like they were *waiting* for that to happen!"

"They *were*. They knew full well Ashbury was gonna be forced home there. Anyone worth their salt would hit her back. The three of them have been keeping her busy with tight teamwork and waiting for their chance to do just this."

Dustin sounded deeply impressed. They had to avoid getting downed, keep her from cottoning on to their plan, and work together to keep her focus going this way and that—it took real finesse. And the timing for their counter had been flawless. You likely couldn't have pulled off the same thing with any other top players in the senior leagues. The Wild Geese were a motley crew of flaky players, and that had paid off for them big-time here.

"Once you've been knocked to the lower sky, it's no easy task regaining speed or altitude. She's lost the greatest strengths a broomrider has, and it's three against one. Even for Ashbury, that's rough. Course, she might still pull through—"

Ashbury was throwing herself into a clash with her foes, heedless of the positional disadvantage. Dustin tore his eyes off her a moment, scanning the other battles on the front line.

"—but it won't be anytime *soon*. This moment here is all Wild Geese."

Broom wars clashes had a hard advantage to whoever landed the first blow. For a very simple reason—moving first meant moving *faster*.

"Aughhh…?!"

"Shit! Why are they attacking?!"

"They're cutting me off! I can't get up to speed!"

The rule every rider knew was working against the Blue Swallows— they'd been *waiting* for Ashbury's rampage to give them openings. But before that could happen, they'd been forced into combat.

"What the heck is Ashbury doing…?!"

"Get back here!"

Even as they fought, her teammates were cursing under their breaths. Getting forced onto the defensive—that was one thing. They'd accounted for the possibility of their opposition starting at Full Attack, so they had their response drilled into their heads. The problem was that Ashbury wasn't *with* them. If she could free herself up, then this was a golden chance to hit their foes from both sides.

Yet, clinging to that idea was dragging them deeper into the bog. An ace-reliant mindset could not handle this Wild Geese onslaught. Their momentum pushed them back, two players went down in rapid succession, and a third player took a heavy hit to their back, lost their balance, and spotted another foe coming in fast. Their doom seemed inescapable—

"Don't *flinch*, people!" a teammate roared, swooping in to the rescue. The Blue Swallows looked startled. They'd all been fighting to protect *him*—the team captain, who should have been waiting on the back lines.

"Honestly, what's wrong with you?! Since when are you useless without Ashbury? Remember our team logo and what it symbolizes!"

A steely glint lit every Swallow's eye. He *knew* the downside of having an ace who was *too good*—and he'd been aware that it could corner them like this. It was a captain's duty to snap his team out of it, and that was why he'd exposed himself on the front lines, setting an example.

"We ain't licked yet, Geese. We ain't a friendly flock like you."

And there was a clear symbol of that attitude—the team logo. Where the Wild Geese and other teams had multiple birds in their logos, the Swallows had only *one*. That solitary swallow symbolized the ultimate ace—and that *every member of the team* should be striving for that level of excellence. A collection of players who valued only their own abilities—that had been the Blue Swallows' ideal since the team's conception.

"Don't *wait* for anyone else! Carve your own path forward! Each of us is a solitary swallow, hell-bent on being the next ace!"

His voice echoed in their ears, reminding them who they were—and banishing their indecision. Vicious smiles appeared on every face, and the unflocked swallows charged into the flock of geese.

*   *   *

"The Blue Swallows are holding up against the Wild Geese's assault! They've been pushed back, but not conquered! Way to stand your ground!"

"That captain's rallying cry did the trick. If morale is back, they won't crumble this easily. There's not a single weak link on their side."

Dustin looked rather pleased, but his smile soon faded. He canceled the amp spell on his wand. He always did when the matches were in a delicate phase to prevent his words altering the flow of the game.

"...But this is the *opposite* of what they thought would happen. They've been forced to focus on the situation at hand—but that can give you tunnel vision. Even a veteran flier will find it tricky to grasp the *whole* of the playing field."

He glanced upward. From the announcer's booth, they could see everything. Including things not visible from the thick of battle.

"And that leaves you blind. Blind enough that no one has noticed a tiny second-year is nowhere to be seen."

On the ground below the battle, as the other catchers braced for plummeters, Oliver alone saw the same thing.

"Yes. *Now*, Nanao."

Yes, right now—Nanao was in the sky far above the fray, about to swoop down into the enemy lines.

"Your head is mine!"

Her aim set, she plunged straight down. Turning her height into speed, faster and faster. At this velocity, the ground was a wall coming up hard, but her eyes saw only the captain's head.

He sensed her coming just before the hit, and his head snapped up—

"Crap—!"

Too late. There was no way he could dodge it now. Nanao's club was swinging with overwhelming speed, aimed right at the Blue Swallows' captain. Her one and only shot at him—so she aimed to down him no matter how he reacted. That thought alone burning in her heart, her mighty swing took her inches from triumph—

"___?!"

—and a flash from the stands blotted her vision.

Nanao had come rocketing out of the sky toward the opponent's captain, but her club missed by a hairbreadth. She barely pulled out of the dive in time, skimming the surface. The crowd gasped aloud.

"Aughhhhhhhh! Hibiya with a stunning surprise attack from on high! A deadly chop right at the captain's head! But she came up empty! Did the nerves get to her?"

"...No."

As Roger roared, Dustin rose to his feet. He upped the amplification on his voice, bellowing at the field.

"Stop the match! Interference! You there! The piece of shit shining light in Hibiya's eyes from the stands! Don't you dare move! You can't fool *my* eyes!"

He pointed right at the stands and saw a speck turn and run.

The horns sounded, stopping the match. The players in flight slowed down.

"Huh? A stoppage?"

"What for? Interference...?"

The three Wild Geese players on Ashbury did the same, gaping at the announcer booth. The Blue Swallows' ace began swooping away, flying off somewhere.

"...Ah?! No, wait!" Melissa yelled. "It's a stoppage!"

*   *   *

"…Tch, overplayed my hand…"

Blending into the tumult of the crowd, he worked his way quickly toward the exit—the "speck" who'd caused the stoppage.

The old student council camp had ordered him to interfere but had no interest in the actual outcome of the match. Whether Ashbury's team or Nanao's won, their grudge was with the two girls whose stunning moves would be all anyone talked about. Their strategy was to ensure that—whatever the outcome—they would embarrass themselves in the process.

Since Ashbury had been locked up through the opening stages, there was little point in bothering her; his attentions had turned to Nanao. Her rapid ascent had made it clear what she planned to do. He had done his best to time things so his interference would go undetected, but that wasn't happening under Dustin's watchful eye. His only remaining option was to get out of dodge before they identified him as the culprit. But as he neared the exit…

"You're not getting away, asshole!"

Several second-years blocked the door—and he knew his plans were foiled.

"We saw the whole thing. It was *your* wand that flashed."

"And you broke into a run when Instructor Dustin called you out."

"How dare you do that to Nanao! What if she'd failed to pull out of the dive in time?!"

Guy, Chela, Pete, and Katie all had their wands drawn, looking furious. The culprit spun around, seeking other exits…but got nowhere. An upperclassman stood before him, wand raised—hair over one eye.

"Your side never surprises. This *classless* behavior did not impress in the previous election, either."

"……!"

Four underclassmen in front of him, Miligan behind—the culprit was trapped with nowhere to go. He drew his athame, hoping to force

his way through the second-years—and a club swung down out of
nowhere, knocking him to the ground.

"Guh?!"

Then a hand shot out, grabbed him by the throat, and squeezed. His
windpipe crushed, he couldn't breathe, much less scream—and he was
hoisted up off his feet.

"*You're* the one who interfered?!"

Hovering in midair on her broom, radiating fury from every inch
of her body—Diana Ashbury. Her bloodlust was so high that even
Miligan took a step back. And the perpetrator learned too late the
fate awaiting anyone who spoiled a broom match while Ashbury was
around.

"...Kah...khhh......!"

"Die."

The bones in his neck creaked. Riders carried no wands or blades,
and their clubs weren't designed to do any lasting damage. The only
way she could kill was with her bare hands. Ashbury was clearly hell-
bent on doing just that. Allowed no resistance or protests, the culprit's
eyes rolled up in his head, his limbs dangling limply—

"Ashbury, that's quite enough."

A girl's voice. Ashbury found a hand on her arm, gently soothing
her fury.

"I am unharmed. My eyes were briefly dazzled, but that is hardly a
concern," Nanao said. "Come, let us resume the match. Our battle has
only just begun."

Shouldering her club, she flashed a grin—and eased Ashbury's
frown.

"...True. Can't waste time on maggots when I'm busy fighting you."

The limp body crashed to the ground. Ashbury spared it no further heed, wheeling back to the field. Arcing across the upper sky, she
barked, "Get this match back underway, refs! In light of the interference, ensure the starting positions favor the Wild Geese!"

The refs quickly conferred and announced the restart positions less than a minute later. Since Nanao's surprise attack would likely have been effective, the positions allowed them to maintain an advantage, and the Wild Geese were starting at a higher altitude. Neither team argued with that, and the players swiftly flew to their start positions—and the horn sounded.

"Here we go again… But let's switch up the dance."

Ashbury was in the same fix she'd been in pre-stoppage with the three Wild Geese members moving to keep her stuck there. One cut in from the side, another joined in based on her reaction, and the third was on standby above, putting pressure on her. A strategy designed to keep her from gaining speed or altitude. Even for Ashbury, no ordinary techniques would get her out of this.

Good thing her techniques were *extraordinary*.

She deflected the first blow with her club. That left her slightly off-balance, and a beat later, the second opponent came swinging in from diagonally behind. Only way to dodge would be to drop down, speeding up—but that would only make her position worse. Bearing down on her, Melissa was certain this placed them one step closer to victory—

"*Huff*—"

—but as Melissa's club swung through, the back before her dropped out of sight—and something grabbed her leg.

"Huh?"

She looked down in shock. Her left foot was in the stirrup, and the tip of a club was hooked onto it. Ashbury dangled from the grip. Deft control of speed and angle made her a weight on whoever her club had snared.

"Wha—?"

"Hah?!"

"You're *kidding*!"

This was a stunt known as the backhook. Logically, during a dog-fight, when both players' speeds were aligned, the rider in front could pull this on their pursuer. As their opponent attacked from behind,

they used the same stall principle as the feather fall to swap places—
and as their pursuer passed them, they used the club to snare them.
But the move itself was far too tricky for even the best broomriders to
pull off—it was a move only *written* about.

"Uh…l-let go! Damn it—"

Melissa sped up, rocking herself right and left, trying to fling her
off. But that club was not just hooked onto her—it was *attached* using
a sword arts technique—Lanoff-style Sticky Edge. She could *try* and
swing her own club, but Ashbury was *behind* her. There was little the
others could do—in such close proximity, any swings they took would
let Ashbury use Melissa as a shield.

And that wasn't even the worst of it. Ashbury wasn't merely dangling
from her feet. She was slowly but steadily stealing her momentum.

"Good enough."

When she'd gained enough speed, she swung the hooked club, passing her. The sideways swipe hit Melissa square in the chest—and her
frantic attempts to escape had left her vulnerable. That hit alone sent
her falling headfirst toward the ground.

"You *asshole*—!"

Curses followed from below, but Ashbury was too busy to listen. The
speed she'd gained from the backhook was more than enough to let
her take on the other two—but there was already a new foe heading her
way from on high.

"Have at thee, Ashbury!"

"Ready for ya."

There was a grin on her face. She'd *known* this was coming. That was
why she'd used the opening moments of the restart to get herself back
to full speed. Feeling the exhilaration bubbling on her skin, Ashbury
threw her entire spirit against the Azian girl.

"Hibiya turned as the match resumed, heading right for Ashbury!
They're really going at it!"

"A wise decision. Her surprise attack failed, and their captain won't make that same mistake again. The best thing she can do is switch targets and try to take Ashbury down. After all, the moment she freed herself from that three-on-one, the Wild Geese no longer had any advantage."

The two of them were fighting far from the main cluster. Until the two battles joined together, this match was still up in the air.

"She downed one of her initial trio; then Hibiya joined in. Still three on one. This is the watershed moment. Can they drop Ashbury before she flips those odds? That'll determine the outcome here."

"Seiaaaaaaaaaaaaaaaaa!"

"Hahhhhhhhhhhhhhhh!"

Their cries echoed across the sky. Their speeds so great, every clash of clubs made sparks fly. And with each clash, Nanao thought anew—how mighty a warrior she fought.

They were *not* an even match. Though it fell to her to land a decisive blow, her teammates were still focused on slowing Ashbury down. Clash into a turn, turn into an ascent—at each phase, they stuck their oars in, and her performance was never at peak. Yet, even under those conditions, the arcs Ashbury traced were never any worse than Nanao's own. It took the three of them to match her at all.

"I couldn't possibly ask for more…!"

Nanao was simply *grateful*. To her fearsome foe, to her worthy allies—to everyone who allowed this moment to be. Without them, she could not fight like this. Could not experience the passion and fulfillment of this instant.

"Seiaaaaaaaaaaaaaaaaaaa!"

Recovering, she turned, rising—and at peak height, she threw herself into a descent. Each stage of that process required the utmost concentration, and yet she thought, *Thus, I must return the favor in kind.* To the teammates she shared a sky with. To the audience watching with

bated breaths. To her catcher, watching from the ground. And to Clifton Morgan, who had asked that she take on Ashbury in *her* sky.

To all who had brought her here.

"——!"

And Ashbury could tell—this girl was driven by feelings for *her own self* as well.

So perhaps…what forced her off her broom on their sixth clash was partly her own doing.

"…Ah—"

It had been a while since she felt this weightlessness. Not quite fear—a sense of loss, like sand flowing between her fingertips. The one who caught her when this happened was no longer down below.

And that sensation drew forth a memory.

"Carve this into your heart, Diana. *This* is your goal."

She was five years old when she'd first held a broom. Her first flight left her feeling exalted, omnipotent. And then her parents showed her the footage.

Inside that crystal was a broomrider in flight. Even at her age, she could tell this rider was going *incredibly* fast. This was nothing like the fun little jaunt she'd just taken. A mage who had devoted her life to flying faster, the fruits of those efforts made manifest. It was beautiful yet terrifying—a *spell* given form.

"Be like her. Be better. Seek what lies beyond this accomplishment."

She agreed before any thoughts crossed her mind. The blood flowing in her veins demanded it. She had never once had a choice. This girl's life had been designed for this, long before her birth. Her body was shorn of all unnecessary weight. Even fully grown, she would lack the ability to bear a child. The Ashbury clan had removed everything not needed from their blood, and she was the result. A single-generation work of art.

Her siblings would carry on that legacy. *Her* task was to fly. To leave everything in her wake, flying where no one else had ever been.

"___!"

And this crystal showed her where that life would lead.

The rider's body *disintegrated*. After that incredible, record-setting flight, the rider's entire body *and* her broom crumbled away like ash in an inferno, scattering across the sky. The ashes carried up into the blue, never to touch the ground again.

The girl sat staring at the sky in the crystal, wondering, *Where did she go?*

She'd done it all and, seconds later, melted into the firmament. There was nothing else to strive for, for the first and last time.

So where had her heart gone?

After Ashbury fell, there were no major turns, and the day closed with the Wild Geese victorious.

At the post-match meeting, Nanao was tossed in the air by her teammates, and when she escaped that, she was mobbed by the Sword Roses. When she finally got away from them, she headed toward the Blue Swallows' training ground, where she found the one she sought flat on her back in the grass.

"Good evening, Ashbury."

"……"

"May I join you?"

Nanao didn't wait for an answer. She sat down by Ashbury, and for a few minutes, neither spoke.

At last, Ashbury broke her sullen silence. "…You've grown even stronger. I never imagined you'd drop me."

"It was hardly my power alone. We honed our strategy, seized the opportunity, and my comrades and I flew as one—and only then could we come close."

"But you're still the one who finished it. If either of the others had come for me there, I know I could've endured."

"And had you not chosen to engage me, you might still have."

Nanao was not being modest. If Ashbury had stayed focused purely on her team's victory, she would never have been in a bullfight with the Azian girl. She could have kept dodging until her teammates came to help, taking the fight back only once her disadvantage was gone. That itself was hardly a simple task—but easier than winning a three-on-one fight.

But Ashbury just shook her head.

"You came in to challenge me. How could I run? That'd just be pathetic."

She snorted; Nanao nodded. Having fought with all her might, she knew better than anyone the shape of this woman's pride.

"…I have things to discuss with you," she said, shifting to her knees.

"Formal," Ashbury said, glancing her way.

"Morgan yet lives. Will you join me tonight and seek him out?"

This hit so hard, she forgot to blink.

And then her mind began churning again. The crystal Leoncio had given her—there'd been a voice in the background she'd heard before, calling that name.

"...Huh. So that was *your* voice."

"?"

"Never mind. So? What about it? He quit being my catcher a long time ago. Whether he's alive or dead—honestly, it makes no difference to me."

The back half might have been less than honest, but the question was real. Leoncio had told her this to rattle her and undermine her match performance. Given his character and the politics of the hour, that was obvious—but the girl before her would never think like that. Ashbury had no clue what could motivate this reveal.

But when her eyes met Nanao's and she found that gaze held true— she knew. This was naught but an act of kindness, done in service of someone she admired.

"To defeat one's self, one must first know one's self. For you, Ashbury—that means Morgan."

"...I *am* me. No one knows me better."

"Nay, Ashbury. You have long averted your eyes from the truth."

"......!"

Ashbury's chest tightened. Nanao was the only person who dared talk like that to her. No words minced, no holds barred. Eyes unclouded, speaking strictly from the heart.

She couldn't dodge it. She felt like a sitting duck. But even so—she shook her head.

"...Maybe you've got a point. But I'm still not going. No matter who says otherwise," she told Nanao. "Seeing him would make me weak. I'd want to *rely* on him. And that would end me. With a heart at peace, I could never reach the fastest realms. I could never get where I need to be."

"Ashbury..."

When Nanao tried to speak again, Ashbury held up a hand, stopping her.

"But I do have a favor to ask, Ms. Hibiya. Two weeks from now—come watch me fly."

"Naturally, I would love to," Nanao said, blinking.

Without realizing it, she had kept her promise to Morgan. Their match today had put the finishing touches on Ashbury's drive.

Ashbury could find nothing lacking. She was sure any more time spent preparing would be a waste, a delay of the inevitable.

"That's the day I fight. The day I ask why Diana Ashbury was born."

Her mind was made up. She would stake every fiber of her being on the spell she sought.

The broomsport world record provided preferential treatment based on times set. This was not a Kimberly preference but a Union one—the better your past achievements, the more accommodations were made for further attempts at the record.

Specifically, and most typically, you could summon top riders at your level for a meet. In other words, you could force other riders to fly along with your record attempt. Naturally, as long as there were people around to ensure the course was regulation and witness the record itself, you could make the attempt alone, but that was purely theoretical; few players aiming for the throne would even consider it. They all knew from experience, and from the history of the sport, that having *rivals* fly the course with you offered clear improvements to your times.

"…Not long now."

Beneath cruelly cerulean skies, Dustin Hedges gazed up at the course rings he himself had ordered polished to perfection. Like the throngs of students here, he was waiting for the star to arrive.

She did not keep them waiting long. Clad in a Blue Swallows uniform, she came strolling out into the arena. A broom on her back, but no club in hand. The sport today needed no weapons. Perhaps as a result, today she seemed disinclined to murder anyone.

Arms folded, Dustin gave her a long look, and she raised a hand in response.

"Here to watch, Instructor?"

"Of course." He snorted. "Who do you think handled negotiations?"

He wasn't exaggerating; it was his hard work that had made this attempt possible. Even with preferential treatment, gathering this many top players on two weeks' notice took some doing. He'd been negotiating not just with the riders themselves but with their schools and coaches, and that had been a real tug-of-war.

Exactly the sort of thing Dustin usually despised, but the moment Ashbury asked him to get the venue ready, he'd thrown himself into it without a word of complaint. No thought in his mind but giving his student the stage she deserved.

"Thanks," Ashbury said with a brief flicker of a smile.

She knew the truth. Her teacher and coach had bent over backward for her. All along, behind the scenes or out in the light of day, he'd been toiling away for her sake.

Awkwardly avoiding his student's gaze, Dustin muttered, "The headmistress ain't coming. Said it would just stress everyone out. But—you know her. She'll be watching from *somewhere*."

Ashbury glanced toward the school building. She'd *better* be watching. The headmistress had relit this fire under her; she *had* to see it through. That *"You've gotten* slow*"* was still ringing in her ears. Ashbury was here to prove that wrong forever, burning the truth into the headmistress's eyes.

But Ashbury never doubted she was watching. The headmistress was out there somewhere—and secure in that belief, she put it out of her mind. Her eyes turned to the faces on the field. Refs from the broomsports committee, timekeepers, catchers, a huge crowd hoping to see history made—and more vital than anyone, the lineup of top players from across the Union.

"The gang's all here."

A row of the world's best riders, all dressed in the liveries of their schools. She'd called them here. Ashbury had the best time among them, but the riders here were the broom races' top twelve. Three were Kimberly students and the remaining nine from other schools. The top reaches of broom racing was a narrow little world. She'd faced every one of them at prior meets; there were no strangers here.

"Faster than I thought. I had money on you pushing it off till next year."

"You've got your sights set? You brought us all here. It better not have been in vain."

They were all glaring at Ashbury. She savored the prickling of her flesh, then issued an ultimatum.

"Thanks for coming out. I want one thing from you: Come after my life, or I'll be taking yours."

And with that, she turned her back and headed for the course itself. The players behind her looked furious...and then started laughing.

"...Ah-ha-ha-ha-ha, and we're doing *her* a favor."

"I came all the way from Lantshire, y'know. And I *hate* Kimberly."

"Sorry. Our girl there ain't got nothing in her head but flying fast."

"Clearly. But still—you can tell she's ready."

The last speaker was the oldest player there. His lips curled arrogantly.

"Don't gripe about her attitude. You're all thinking the same thing. Everyone else here is to make *you* better."

The exact same smile appeared on every face. Of course. They weren't the audience. This was a *meet*. Every one of them had a shot at the record. That's why they'd come. Historically, players invited like this *had* actually set new records—and more than a few times.

Ashbury's attempt had them all feeling competitive and motivated. And Dustin knew it.

"No one's missing. Nothing comes up, we'll start on time. First three, on the course."

He drew his white wand, waving at three players. Two of them boarded their brooms and flew off, but Ashbury first did a flyby of the stands.

"Ms. Hibiya, hold these."

She took her wand and athame off her waist and handed them to Nanao where she sat with the Sword Roses. This pair was the hallmark of a mage and the final anchor on a broomrider. Given only to one you trusted—Nanao clutched them tight.

"...Mm. They are safe with me."

"Good."

Ashbury headed up to the start line. Three riders were waiting above.

"All players in position!" Dustin roared, his voice amplification active. "Thirty seconds! Countdown will start at ten."

He took a small sphere from his pocket and had it hover at the tip of his wand. Horns and whistles were never piercing enough, and signaling with a spell was at the mercy of the chanter's voice. Broomsport events had long made use of these specialized burst orbs. The count itself was done by a nearby ref, and Dustin pumped magic into the orb in time with it.

"...Three, two, one—zero!"

A crack echoed across the heavens. And three shooting stars took off.

Broom races were a very simple sport. The course was a series of rings in the air, and the players flew through them in order. As long as no one skipped a ring or obstructed another player, the winner was determined just like any ordinary race—by whoever reached the final goal first.

Since this was a world record event, it used a standardized course, an extremely orthodox layout involving three straightaways, four corners, and two windings, and they'd compete for time on three laps. Unlike ground-based courses, this one turned in three dimensions, so the riders were forced to make tight turns up, down, right, and left.

"Hoo...!"

"Phew—!"

Their launch speeds had already been tremendous. Their acceleration down the first straightaway made the crowd doubt their eyes. They hit the corner on a line that suggested they'd run a con on inertia, and they blazed through the winding that followed with dizzying maneuvers. The first lap was over inside a minute, and they headed into the next with no loss of speed.

Everyone here could ride a broom, but most had never seen the top riders fly before. And all thought the same thing—this was *insane*.

"First down! Time?"

"2:26:47!" the timekeeper called.

"Starting in the twenty-six-second block?" Dustin muttered. "Not bad. Second try! Everyone but Ashbury swap out! Next two, take your places!"

The riders flying with Ashbury swapped out on the regular, and the first ten minutes went by with tension rising.

"…Ten-minute break! Come on back, Ashbury," Dustin called.

It was part of his job to make sure they got the rest they needed. She collapsed on a bench he had waiting for her.

"…*Huff, huff…*"

"Drink up. Sip at a time. Like it's nectar from a flower."

He handed her a potion with a straw stuck in, and she gulped away. He'd made it just for her, from the ingredients to its viscosity. She caught her breath and focused on recovering her strength.

"…You're on the right track," Dustin said. "Here's where the fight really begins. Don't let your focus waver."

"The hell do you think you're talking to…?"

Her canine punctured the straw. Dustin knew he'd picked the right words. This *was* where the fight started.

"Three, two, one—zero!"

After that brief break, they headed into the fourth attempt, the crowd watching with bated breath. There were benches behind them, but no one took a seat.

"…I can't…breathe…"

"Don't force yourself to watch, Katie."

The curly-haired girl had a hand to her face, taking short, shallow breaths. Oliver looked rather alarmed. She was far too empathetic; this spectacle was a bit too much for her.

"…This is a broom races world record attempt," he explained. "These riders have trained for this day, trimmed everything else away—they're all flying past their own limits. The intensity is so high, it's not at all unusual for racers to die in the attempt. Not even from a fall, just dying in midflight."

"It is not an event you *enjoy* watching. Yet, that is what makes it so compelling," Chela added. "What is the nature of a mage's life? What does it mean to risk your life for something? The way they fly forces us to ponder those great riddles."

She never once took her eyes off the fliers. Oliver had his own thoughts on her comments and glanced toward the Azian girl at his side.

"…Think she can do it, Nanao? Break the record?"

He wasn't sure why, but he felt like only she could give an accurate read. And it took her a long moment to respond.

"………The time is not yet ripe."

Six more attempts. Thirty minutes of excruciating flight and a third short rest. Ashbury reeled to the bench, barely conscious, and Dustin grabbed her roughly.

"What's wrong with you, Ashbury? Is that all you got? Is that your limit?!"

"……Hah…… Hah……"

Dustin was desperately trying to keep the last light in her eyes from going out. She couldn't afford to pass out here—that would spell the end to her concentration and the end of her attempt. They would never again assemble a lineup like this. Even if they did, it would be after Ashbury's abilities had peaked. This was her shot. The one chance she had at achieving her goal.

"I know it isn't! You're not done yet! You can't be…!"

Before he knew it, there were tears rolling down his cheeks. There was nothing he could do to help her here; he was up against the hard limit of what a coach could offer. His voice reached her ears but seemed so far away; despite his best efforts, her mind was slipping into darkness.

"Gah-ha-ha, you finally made a teacher cry!"

Ashbury's eyes snapped open. That distinctive laugh was like a kick in the pants to her flagging spirits.

"Mor...gan...?"

Her blurred vision and bleary mind both snapped into focus. She was lying on a bench, and a man was looming over it, looking down at her.

"...Looks like we got here in time. Barely."

This came from the smaller man next to him: Kevin Walker, the Survivor. He was helping the larger man stand: her catcher, Clifton Morgan. In the flesh.

"Will you not pay Ashbury a visit?"

It was the night they had been attacked on the second layer. Morgan had come to save them, and Nanao had sat face-to-face with him, pleading with him to change his mind.

"I am aware of the difficulties. Yet—this cannot stand. Ashbury is wagering all that she is and has been and yet finds herself unable to commit the last reserves of her strength."

She sounded very certain. And that got his attention.

"...Why do you think that?"

"She has lost the place her heart lies. That is separate from one's goal—but is a thing we all need when we are racing toward a far-off destination. A journey with no home to return to is little more than drifting."

Nanao had lost her home to war. Though brought to Kimberly, she had spent a long time adrift before finding a new place with the Sword

Roses. That's why she knew. Though Ashbury herself might be loath to admit it—this was what she needed.

"Ashbury has deemed the desire for a home a weakness and is attempting to dismiss it. But as long as she is human, that can never be. Yet, as a result, I fear I may not be able to bring her here. Much to my chagrin."

Nanao's fists were clenched tight. She got down on her knees, bowing her head low and placing her palms on the ground. A gesture from a different culture, yet the polished movements and the intent behind them were painfully clear. This stance was the highest expression of sincerity that she possessed.

"Clifton Morgan, I beseech you. Step once more into the halls of our campus—for the sake of the broomrider you love."

He'd thought about it for days and finally acquiesced to her plea.

"I can't do much. Can barely hold a wand. I'm just part of the scenery."

It'd been so long since they'd seen each other, and he was just putting his condition in plain words. There was a reason he hadn't left the labyrinth. He was preparing for the worst, of course, but also because as long as he remained in the labyrinth with its high magic-particle density, the tír fire's ravaging was somewhat suppressed.

On the second layer, he'd still been able to fight. But on the first layer, that had swiftly deteriorated, and by the time he'd reached the school, he couldn't even walk without assistance. He'd known this would happen; that was why he'd asked for Kevin Walker's help. The Survivor had agreed immediately. They'd had plenty of problems along the way but had somehow made it in time.

"…But will that change anything?" Morgan asked, looking right at her.

Ashbury slowly peeled herself off the bench.

"Dunno. Maybe not."

Yet, despite those words, there was a smile on her lips. She got back on her broom and flew away. The next pair of competitors joined her at the start line. Feeling a change in the wind, Dustin glanced at the ref and timekeeper, then readied a burst orb.

"Three, two, one—zero!"

The countdown to the tenth attempt. Three stars shot across the sky. And the start alone sent a stir through the crowd.

"Yo, is she...?"

"She's flying differently."

"Yeah, gaining more speed out the gate."

The racers left on the ground could all tell. And their read was soon obvious to everyone—Ashbury had pulled away from the competition. As she tore out of the corner into the bend, the riders gasped again.

"Is that shit real?!"

"It can't be—at *that* speed?"

"This ain't funny. It's like water coursing down a canal!"

Their faces were a fright: impressed but also jealous as all hell. Her strong, aggressive maneuvers had always been there—but the tension behind them was gone. She was no longer desperately trying to push something out of mind, and the power that gave her was compelling her onward. She could fly *straight*.

"...Nanao, is she—?" Oliver began.

Nanao nodded. "*Now* the time is ripe."

He'd suspected as much. Nanao had always seen what he saw now.

At last, Ashbury realized the truth. She had never been afraid of falling *or* dying.

The pressure of the incoming age cutoff, the fear that she might not set a new record before then—neither of those was what had ravaged her heart so. In fact, she'd always been certain she could do it. She *knew* she could put the work of a lifetime to the test and reach the realm beyond.

2:20:87.

The thing that scared her—to her chagrin—was what lay *after* that. Running a course at the cost of her life, surpassing the limits of her flesh, and after that—the idea planted in her head by the footage her parents had shown her. That scant few seconds *before* her body disintegrated—*that* was what she feared.

2:22:16.

She was certain those seconds would be devastating. Once she'd fulfilled the duty Ashbury blood demanded of her, reached the realm she strove for—what would be left to her? Where would her heart go? She feared she would vanish without knowing, without direction, her heart adrift in an empty sky. Even as a child, she'd been certain that moment would arrive—and she had been terrified of it.

2:23:58.

What she'd needed was *somewhere to go* when that time arrived.

There had always been just one option. She hadn't wanted to admit it. Relying on someone she'd lost—that was a weakness, and she was so mad at herself for it, she'd unconsciously shifted the goalposts. Told herself having someone like that would stop her from achieving results. Told herself he was long since dead. She let those thoughts loop through her mind, attaching convincing logic to them—until she had herself fooled.

But he'd been clinging to life, holed up in the labyrinth for two whole years.

And she'd been unable to deceive that nosy samurai. That girl was the kind of dumb that saw right through you.

And the moment the two of them met—that was the time for it all to catch up with her.

2:24:37.

She was through the winding, into the final straightaway. At speeds this great, her peripherals were gone. All she could see was the final ring. And she was fine. She wasn't scared. Once she passed it, her heart would not be lost.

She knew exactly where to go.

He was waiting for her down below.

"…Heh."

She was bound for what lay beyond that ring.

There was nothing left to fear. No more reason to hesitate. To the fastest speed she'd seen and one step beyond—

2:24:98.

The timekeeper's count stopped on that figure. A silence settled over the arena.

"…You did it…," Dustin gasped. A moment later, tears fell down his cheeks. "………You're the fastest ever, Ashbury."

When those words echoed through the arena, the crowd leaped to their feet with a titanic roar. The judge, the catchers, the timekeeper—everyone raised their hands to the sky. Only the riders who'd flown with her did anything else: Their eyes went to the skies above, wrestling with the tumult within. This was a key moment in *all* their lives.

"…She did it, Morgan. She actually did it," Walker whispered. Morgan was still leaning on his shoulder. They'd feared Ashbury would die setting the record like the previous holder had, but she'd clearly escaped that fate—she was still looping through the air above, gradually slowing herself down.

Eyes on her and her alone, Morgan croaked, "…Gah-ha… Always did…have a simple mind. One change to the scenery, and she—"

But even as he grumbled, deep down—he was glad he'd come. Grateful to the Survivor for bringing him here and the kids who'd talked him into it. Glad his final task had helped one great broomrider.

"——!"

And even as the thought crossed his mind, the thing keeping him together snapped.

"…Whoops… N-not good…"

His body shook with an unnatural heat. Uncanny flames spurted out, escaping from within. Walker saw that and gasped.

"Morgan!"

"…Get away from me, Walker!"

He gave the Survivor a mighty shove. With the last of his strength, Morgan stumbled away from the crowds. He'd had his eye on that space from the start: toward the center of the course, where no one now flew. He'd fulfilled his purpose.

"……Morgan, you're…," Dustin said; one look and he knew what this meant.

A safe distance away, Morgan turned back, his last smile on his lips.

"……Sorry, everyone. Looks like my time's up," he said. "Gah-ha… Instructor……handle the cleanup, plea—"

His voice died in a croak. The flames around him billowed higher.

"Morgaaaaaaaaan!"

What followed was a massive, raging sphere of fire. Flames lashing so high they swallowed the ring above, like a sun upon the ground.

"Waugh…?!"

"Yiiikes…!"

"Get back! Don't touch that fire!" Oliver yelled, pushing his friends away. The man's time had come. Oliver had known that was possible, but that knowledge didn't make it any easier. "…Morgan has been consumed by the spell. That's the tír fire he summoned and failed to control."

He gritted his teeth. Those flames moved as if they had a will of their own, and just feeling that heat made his skin crawl. Every instinct screaming this fire was *wrong*. It was literally not of this world. It had lurked within Clifton Morgan's body since he'd summoned it from Luftmarz and was now rampaging out of him, seeking release into their world and turning its host's mana into kindling.

"Sadly, there's nothing we can do here. Leave this to the faculty and evacuate—"

He pushed his friends farther away, forcing himself to make the rational choice. But the Azian girl was already on her broom, rising high into the sky.

"Nanao?!"

"Escort them to safety, Oliver. She's calling for me."

She had a wand and an athame clutched to her chest. Before Oliver could stop her, she was headed to their owner, as fast as her broom could carry her.

She'd just waved a hand, knowing that would do the trick. And she wasn't wrong—not twenty seconds later, Nanao was in the sky by her side.

"…Are these what you seek, Ashbury?"

"Yeah. Glad you're quick on the uptake."

Nanao held out both, but Ashbury took only the athame, leaving the empty scabbard in the girl's hands. She no longer needed it.

"Do you require anything further from me?"

"Nope. Getting this to me is plenty. You go back to your friends."

She waved her off. Nanao's lips tightened. Ashbury noticed that—and smiled.

"Don't give me that look. I've gotta be his Final Visitor. He's my catcher."

Nanao's head was down. She forced back all else she wished to say and nodded.

"…Very well."

By the time she spoke, the matter was settled within her. She looked right at Ashbury, her expression now unclouded and cheery—as if seeing a friend off on their journey.

"Enjoy your journey, Lady Ashbury. 'Twas a pleasure knowing you."

"Likewise, Ms. Hibiya."

Ashbury put a lot in those few words. And on that note, they parted. Nanao turned in the air and flew back to the ground. Ashbury alone remained above. A whim washed over her, and she laid a palm on the handle of the broom.

"Sorry, you're gonna have to come with me. But you don't mind, do you? You'll be flying with *me*."

It had been a long time since she'd spoken to it. She'd been with this broom ever since her first flight. As she strove to be better, faster—the division between them had faded. It became a part of her. Her broom felt the same and would hardly argue that point now. It flew where she wanted to fly. That was all. To Diana Ashbury's broom, that was always the best flight around.

All preparations complete, she ascended upon high, gazing down at the blazing fireball below. Even from this towering height, she could feel the heat of it. As more time passed, the walls of fire expanded farther. And beyond them, she could still see her man.

"...Sheesh, so *demanding*. You finally show yourself around here, and *this* happens."

She snorted. He never had been remotely considerate. She had a laundry list of gripes saved up. Especially the part where he'd gone two whole years without letting her air them.

"Don't worry. I'll be right with you."

She was high enough now. She made her turn and aimed for the ground. Her sights set on the center of the fireball—she dropped like a stone.

"Ashbury—!"

Dustin saw her coming and let out a scream. He knew exactly what she was doing and knew he had no way of stopping her. This was all he *could* do.

He might be one of the best riders in the world, but brooms were his sole area of expertise. His skill set gave him no way of quickly subsuming a tír incursion of this scale. His one chance would have been to cut Morgan's head off before the spell consumed him, but the depth of his emotions had stayed his hand. He'd been Morgan's instructor, too. And Morgan had been Ashbury's catcher. Even as his student was consumed by the spell, he'd hoped there was a way to save him. All while knowing perfectly well there was none.

And the real problem lay beyond. If Morgan's salvation was impossible, then Dustin needed to deal with the fallout—given time, there were any number of approaches. Even now, other teachers would be racing toward them, aware of the issue at hand. The headmistress herself would almost certainly be here within ten seconds. The rest of the faculty would contain the incursion before Dustin himself took any action.

But that was *too late*.

He could not wait. Ten seconds was an eternity with the world's fastest broomrider—!

Less than two seconds into her descent, Ashbury's body would be enveloped in those flames. At the three-second mark, she'd hit the center of the fireball, and mere moments later, there would be nothing left of her. She was perfectly aware of that fate.

Ashbury was a broomrider. She knew no means of taming tír fire. She'd never even considered attempting it. To her eyes, the matter was a simple one: the *distance* to her destination and the *time* it would take to reach it.

She knew her catcher stood at the heart of that fireball. The tír fire was fueled by his mana, so that was a given. If the host died, the flames could no longer absorb his strength. In other words, even consumed by the spell, Morgan himself was the *core* of this phenomenon.

So stopping it was easy. If she could reach him, she could end this.

She need merely pierce his heart. And before her own body burned away, at that.

"Ngh—"

She plunged into the flames. The heat grew astronomically worse.

In the first instant, her eyes burned away, and she was blind. A moment later, all sounds disappeared, and then all sensation from her skin was lost. She heard nothing, saw nothing, each of her five senses vanishing in turn as she plunged through the inferno and into darkness—yet none of that rattled her at all.

Her left hand stayed locked upon the handle of her broom. Her body leaned forward. The tip of the athame in her right hand aimed dead ahead.

The damage was no detriment. Seen or unseen, she would reach her goal.

To the one she loved the most. Her heart now freed from the duty of her blood, she was headed to her final abode.

To those burly arms that had held her so painfully tight.

"_____!"

Her blade hit something. The impact traveled up her carbonized arm, shattering it, and kept going through her entire body. It was over in an instant. She knew she'd reached her limit.

In the moment before her mind gave way to darkness, she felt those big arms catch her.

The swirling flames abated. They died down so swiftly, it was as if that madness had never existed to begin with.

With the fire gone, only a large, scorched circle remained. What had been there had burned itself out, leaving nothing behind but pure white ash. And the mages who'd witnessed it watched, stunned.

"____"

"......"

Nanao's tears fell in silence. Oliver's eyes were closed in reverence.

He found himself asking—where had their hearts gone?

None could know the answer. But wherever it might be, he knew one thing for sure.

They were there together.

Epilogue

Even as that uproar was unfolding above, a boy was wandering through the paths of the labyrinth's first layer, humming to himself.

"~~♪~~~♪~~~♪"

Yuri Leik, self-proclaimed transfer student. He now spent the bulk of his time exploring the school and the labyrinth.

This often put him in danger, but that proved no impediment to his boundless curiosity. There were things down there he'd never seen, never heard, never smelled, never touched, never tasted—and a thirst for that *unknown* drove him onward. Where that urge came from, even he himself didn't know.

"…Mm?"

Yuri came to a halt. There was a figure approaching him down the passage dressed in baggy blue robes, like a philosopher. Yuri folded his arms, trying to place the new arrival.

"Ummmmm… Oh, right! I remember! Instructor Demitrio. What a coincidence seeing you here! What brings you—?"

But mid–friendly ramble, the man's hand clamped around the boy's face.

"Altum somnum."

With that incantation, Yuri's body jerked—and his hands went limp.

Demitrio kept his grip on the boy's face, closing his eyes and standing perfectly still. As if siphoning something through the grip.

"......"

"Your soul split never fails to impress, Instructor Demitrio. No matter how many times I see it."

A dapper voice echoed from above. A man with luxuriant ringlets stood suspended from the ceiling: Kimberly's part-time lecturer Theodore McFarlane.

"You said you split your soul into two halves—'ignorance' and 'knowledge,' was it? I would never have imagined that possible without seeing it with my own eyes. An entirely new type of familiar."

Theodore hopped down from the ceiling, standing next to the astronomy instructor. As he landed, Demitrio released Yuri, and the boy landed flat on his back, unconscious. The ringlet instructor grinned down at the boy's comatose face, innocent in slumber.

"Rather a cute splinter this time. Makes me wonder—were *you* ever like this?"

"...The appearance is arbitrary, but the personality was once mine. He is me, minus my accumulated knowledge and experience."

Demitrio's tone was flat. His eyes might be gazing upon a part of himself, but they were possessed of that specific ennui that came from knowing *too much*.

"Knowledge is bondage. With it comes loss. There are things only the ignorant can see, ask, or touch. This world is filled with such irony. And this fact holds true even here at Kimberly," Demitrio intoned. "Thus, have I sought out ignorance. I gained the knowledge that it brings as a step on the path to true omniscience."

Theodore returned a nod of utmost respect. How best to approach the problem—on that point, this philosopher's thoughts were unlike any other mage's.

"These innocent eyes will soon discover the truth beyond Darius's and Enrico's deaths. The true nature of our enemy."

*   *   *

After a slumber of indeterminate length, Yuri found himself lying on the hard ground.

"...Hmm...?"

He scratched his head blearily, sitting up. Then he looked around and realized he'd been asleep in the labyrinth. How had that happened? He had no memory of it.

"...Huh. That's weird! What am I *doing*?"

Although the doubt crossed his mind, he didn't pursue it. He was soon walking again—any notion that something was amiss instantly forgotten. His mind was carefully tuned to do just that.

He was Demitrio's splinter, a product of a soul split—but he was no spy. Yuri himself was unaware of his mission. His actions were unrestrained by any knowledge, his views and perspectives available only in his ignorance. And with that, he would solve the mysteries lurking within Kimberly's walls.

Yuri Leik, transfer student. The explorer with innocent eyes. His role: *the detective.*

END

Afterword

Good evening. This is Bokuto Uno. The curtain has fallen on a tumultuous second year.

Investigations and elections. Teachers and students alike scheming away—and she alone paid it all no heed, pursuing only her own path of sorcery. Mages who bore witness to it will not forget how bright she shone.

A shooting star across the sky and the place her trajectory led. A rider and catcher the school could be proud of. Their story ends here.

Yet, new ripples spread, their outcome unclear. Elections, feuds, and a detective—Kimberly has far too many dynamics at play. Where will they take us? How will they mingle? No one can say for sure. All they can do is hold fast to the belief that they will emerge victorious.

The scent of the next spell lingers all around. Watch your step closely, lest you find yourself plummeting into that abyss.

HAVE YOU BEEN TURNED ON TO LIGHT NOVELS YET?

86—EIGHTY-SIX, VOL. 1-10

In truth, there is no such thing as a bloodless war. Beyond the fortified walls protecting the eighty-five Republic Sectors lies the "nonexistent" Eighty-Sixth Sector. The young men and women of this forsaken land are branded the Eighty-Six and, stripped of their humanity, pilot "unmanned" weapons into battle...

Manga adaptation available now!

WOLF & PARCHMENT, VOL. 1-6

The young man Col dreams of one day joining the holy clergy and departs on a journey from the bathhouse, Spice and Wolf. Winfiel Kingdom's prince has invited him to help correct the sins of the Church. But as his travels begin, Col discovers in his luggage a young girl with a wolf's ears and tail named Myuri who stowed away for the ride!

Manga adaptation available now!

SOLO LEVELING, VOL. 1-5

E-rank hunter Jinwoo Sung has no money, no talent, and no prospects to speak of—and apparently, no luck, either! When he enters a hidden double dungeon one fateful day, he's abandoned by his party and left to die at the hands of some of the most horrific monsters he's ever encountered.

Comic adaptation available now!

The Detective Is Already Dead

When the story begins without its hero

Kimihiko Kimizuka has always been a magnet for trouble and intrigue. For as long as he can remember, he's been stumbling across murder scenes or receiving mysterious attaché cases to transport. When he met Siesta, a brilliant detective fighting a secret war against an organization of pseudohumans, he couldn't resist the call to become her assistant and join her on an epic journey across the world.

...Until a year ago, that is. Now he's returned to a relatively normal and tepid life, knowing the adventure must be over. After all, the detective is already dead.

Volume 1 available wherever books are sold!

YEN
ON
YenPress.com

TANTEI HA MO, SHINDEIRU. Vol. 1
©nigozyu 2019
Illustration: Umibouzu
KADOKAWA CORPORATION